I0663101

THE DEFENDER

#10

THE
GOOD FIGHT

Books by Jerry Ahern

The Survivalist Series

The Defender Series

They Call Me the Mercenary Series

THE DEFENDER

#10

THE
GOOD FIGHT

JERRY AHERN

SPEAKING VOLUMES, LLC

NAPLES, FLORIDA

2012

THE DEFENDER

#10 THE GOOD FIGHTP

ISBN 978-1-61232-315-2

For those men and women throughout human history who have valued personal freedom more than personal safety—sometimes unpopular, never anachronistic, seldom remembered . . .

Chapter One

*T*he rods—either steel or heavy-gauge aircraft aluminum, but inflexible even when as many men as could lay hands on one at once tugged with all their might—were set two inches apart. Throughout grammar school, high school, and even at West Point, Barnabas Wood's classmates had always made fun of his nose, calling it everything from an albino cucumber to a short elephant trunk to a misplaced penis, taunting him with names ranging from Pinocchio to Cyrano (depending on their degree of literacy) because of its abnormal length and awkward symmetry. Yet when he pressed his long nose between the bars, sometimes his nose was just long enough that he could get a whiff of the real air his fellow prisoners were denied by their more conventionally handsome physiognomies.

But most of the time the slipstream flowing around the cattle car in which he was imprisoned only carried back the smells of the cattle car just ahead, as bad as the air within the one he occupied.

Because of these occasional breaths of untainted oxygen his proboscus afforded him, he lay stuporous less of the time than many of the other seventy-three officers within the pen on wheels. And as a result he was able to ascertain with a good degree of certainty that he and the others were traveling toward no real destination at all, merely moving in what—in every way but geometric—could be called a circle.

The fresh air made him light-headed again, but that was attributable to the nausea. Yet he kept his nose between the bars because the air was vital to maintaining whatever degree of good health was possible under the circumstances; and he was watching for the Marlboro Man billboard. Someone had painted over the horse's rear end ROMAN MAKOWSKI.

Like a lot of the men with him, Barnabas Wood, Jr., had been unable to keep anything down for at least the last two days.

He saw the billboard. His great circle–route theory was once again confirmed. And seeing Roman Makowski compared to a horse's ass brought a smile to his lips, diverted his thoughts from his own misery for almost as long as a second.

Wood turned away from the bars as the odor from the car ahead assailed him worse than the unflushed-toilet smell within his own prison. There were two chemical toilets, one at either end of the car. The men aboard the car were allowed to empty these periodically but could do so only when the train was stopped. The train had not stopped for better than a day.

Suspended from the roof at the center of the car were two five-gallon plastic containers of water, these air-pressure fed. As water was tapped from a container, the container collapsed partially. Both containers were close to ninety-percent empty, so there was no water to use to clean men who were so sick they had dirtied themselves.

The constant motion and irregularly offered and disgusting, spoiled-tasting rations aggravated the conditions aboard the car still more. Not a man riding the car could truthfully say he hadn't vomited at least once within the last twelve hours.

The ranking officer, a marine lieutenant colonel named Young, had organized a rotating detail to push what could be disposed of through the openings at the base of the bars, but this could be done only when the train was going slowly enough that the material would not get caught in the slipstream and be washed into the car behind, adding to the misery of the men there. Some of the officers aboard the car were excused from this duty because they were already ill or, in a few cases, had minor wounds that might become still more infected than these already were. Some, like Wood himself, volunteered for the detail. It was something to do and, unlike the others, he could always get his whiff of air.

Whispered rumors maintained that one of the cars held female officers, but there was no evidence to support this. It was also said that there were several such trains as this. The verifiable facts—Wood reviewed them in his mind—were that officers from all branches of the United States military, including coast guard, were represented here; senior noncoms from all branches were being held in similar cars (this confirmed when contact was established with the car behind); and that no one knew why any of this was happening. There were plenty of guesses, most centering on President Roman Makowski trying to seize control of the country by force after having completely suspended constitutional government, incarcerating duly commissioned officers from key units only to replace them with Hobart Townes's hand-picked scum from the Presidential Strike Force.

Colonel Young stepped over the semicomatose navy lieutenant commander lying beside Wood and started to sit down. Wood began to get up. "As you were, Lieutenant."

"Thank you, sir."

"What time do you think it is, Wood?"

"I'm not sure, sir, but I figure it's a little after seven. I tried to judge the sunset, but it's a little hard the way the terrain rolls."

"After seven sounds good. I was talking to a man who knows about you. I understand you represented the Point in several track events."

"Yes, sir. I was never much good as a miler though."

"How about the four forty and eight eighty—the sprints?"

"Yes, sir." Wood nodded, eager for the chance to talk about something fresh, different. "I was always pretty good at those." And he laughed. "I remember they used to say I did so well because this schnoz of mine"—and Wood tapped at his nose—"this thing acted like a kind of snow plow for the air, cutting down my wind resistance."

"Have you kept up with the running?"

"I'm Airborne Ranger Infantry, sir. Six miles a day every day, sir, more when I'm on duty. Plus then I do some sprints for fitness."

The colonel smiled. "Some of us—Major Wilton, Lieutenant Commander Corrigan, like that—have been cooking up a little idea. Wanted to see if you want to get involved." Major Wilton was the ranking army officer, Corrigan the ranking naval man. "It's not the sort of thing we'll order you to do, Wood. How are you feeling?"

Wood looked at Colonel Young's slightly yellow-cast face in the intermittent light. "Pretty good, sir. All things considered."

"You seem to be among the healthiest and you're probably the fastest. We're planning an escape. But only for one man. We want you to be that man."

"But, sir—"

"Let me finish, Lieutenant." And Colonel Young

grinned a little. "I admit that nose might make a perfect target—"

Wood laughed, looked down at his hands.

"But all kidding aside, I'll outline the mission and you can accept or reject. No one will think less of you and, if we get out of here, this won't go on your record if you refuse."

"Yes, sir. I understand. What am I supposed to do?"

"A number of us have been discussing this on and off. And we've arrived at the conclusion that nobody knows we're here aboard this train. Our wives, our families, God knows what they know. But the American people can't know that this is happening. Somebody has to get out and tell them. With those guards on top of the cars, a mass break might get a bunch of us away, but so many of the men here are already too sick to run fast. Too many of them would get killed.

"But one man," the colonel persisted, "would have a chance at breaking away while the rest of us created a diversion. I have no idea where we are—"

"I think we're near Metro, sir. When I was a kid, we traveled to Metro several times on my dad's business. He was a plumbing contractor. Got me interested in architecture a little. Sometimes when we're circling I keep thinking that I've seen some of the buildings in the skyline before. I think it is Metro."

"I don't know where you should go, whether it's Metro or not." Colonel Young nodded. "I don't know who you can trust. But you have to find somebody. Get the truth out, then hide yourself and see what happens. Another reason you're the perfect man—you're not married, right?"

"No, sir. I'm not." He had a girl, but if he told the colonel anything about her it might alter the colonel's decision. And somebody had to get word out. He was healthier still than most of the other officers aboard the car, and he could run. "I want to do it, sir."

"You don't have to, Wood."

"Begging the colonel's pardon, but yes, I do, sir. In another twenty-four hours some of the men here are going to be dying. And if that story that's been circulating is true, that there's a car like this loaded up with women officers, well . . ."

"You're a brave man and a good officer, Lieutenant. And if we do get out of this, well, you ever feel like getting into the Corps, well"—and the colonel grinned, his face looking more yellow than ever—"we really are still looking for a few good men."

Wood smiled. "Thank you, sir."

"The next time we stop. Now get some rest. How are your boots?"

"They're fine, sir."

"Rest—and that's an order."

"Yes, sir."

Lieutenant Colonel Young stood up, pushing down on Wood's shoulder to keep him from standing.

Barnabas Wood turned his face toward the bars again. The stench was overpowering.

He closed his eyes. The colonel was right. He needed to rest. And there'd be time for some limbering-up exercises before he made the run.

The part about not having a wife— He'd had a date lined up with Sandi, but the men from the Presidential Strike Force had grabbed him just as he came off duty. Did she think he'd stood her up, backing away maybe because they'd talked about marriage?

Had she called the base? What did she get told? *Lieutenant Wood can't be disturbed now, ma'am.* Or *Lieutenant Wood left word that if you called just to say he was sorry . . . No, ma'am, no other message . . . No, ma'am, he can't be reached . . . Not tomorrow, either, ma'am.*

If Sandi kept calling enough, would they come for her?

When he closed his eyes, he saw Sandi in a cattle car like this, other women—wives, fiancées, steady girls, mothers, and sisters—penned up with her, some of them crying, some of them just staring off hopelessly.

So Wood opened his eyes, scrunched up close to the bars again, trying for another breath of air.

Sandi called his nose *unique*, once even *regal*, and both of them had laughed. It was just big and long and ugly.

Sandi used to kiss the tip of it.

Sprints had always been his specialty, and this one would be his fastest ever.

Chapter Two

*T*he Big Ugly One's full-tang black linen Micarta paneled grip was tight in Rose Shepherd's gloved right fist. David had polished her sentry-removal skills with her; but as he'd told her then, it was never a job anyone felt comfortable with. You got so close, he told her, that you could smell the guy's underarms or his shoes and when you finally got him, smelling his breath was the most pleasant of the possible odors in store for you. She'd already known the thing about the odors. Sometimes—and there didn't seem to be any rhyme or reason to it—the man would wet his pants, or worse.

Rose Shepherd was close enough now, started rising to her full height as she crossed the last few yards in long—she hoped silent—strides.

A twig she hadn't seen snapped under her left boot.

The Presidential Strike Force trooper started to turn around.

Rose Shepherd broke into a dead run.

He raised the M-16 as he half pivoted toward her, his mouth opening to sound an alarm.

"Shit," she snarled under her breath.

She jumped onto his right shoulder and back, her body weight driving him forward. She could feel his knees start to buckle as her gloved left hand clamped over his mouth.

The Big Ugly One. She punched the six inches of quarter-inch-thick 440C barstock into the trooper's carotid artery and out his larynx as they fell together to the ground, the blade all the way through to the brass guard, the point of the knife piercing into the ground beneath them as she snapped his head back. The body was spiked into the dirt at the throat.

Rose Shepherd lay there trying to remember how to breathe.

If David had seen this, he would have told her that her sentry-removal technique had been less than textbook-perfect this time.

David Holden averted his eyes, forcing his consciousness to focus on the texture of a dried, half-crumpled maple leaf on the ground near his feet, mentally tracing its vein pattern.

There was a school of thought that held that if one concentrated on another human being long enough, the subject of that concentration could somehow feel eyes on him and would turn toward their source.

At the distance at which the terrain forced David Holden to observe the man, the only way to take him out would be to shoot him. And that would raise an alarm. There were some men, of course, who could throw a knife with uncanny accuracy. David Holden was not one of these.

His fist tightened on the butt of the Defender as he inhaled, stood, then sprinted toward the man. In his mind Holden still saw the fragile, failing beauty of the leaf.

Gloved left hand over the mouth of the Presidential Strike Force man at the instant of body contact, snapping the head back, right knee smashing upward into the small of the back at the spine, the knife's primary edge raking left to right across the exposed throat.

Blood sprayed as the artery opened, but Holden wore safety glasses and his mouth and nose were covered with a bandana, his hands gloved.

One couldn't be too careful these days when it came to blood.

Rose Shepherd dropped to her knees at the base of the high-rise chain-link fence, shrugging out of the teardrop-shaped day pack. The grappling hooks. She secured the center one first into the fence at about two feet, hitch ball level with the ground, then the one to its right and the one to the left, her left hand grabbing up the pack, her right feeding out the water-ski rope as she edged away from the fence. . . .

Holden had the first hundred feet of the rope coiled out, but dropped into the ditch paralleling the roadway as the command car rolled past. He exhaled, looking over the lip of the depression in the predawn gray and recognizing the face of the camp commander from the description given him by Lem Parrish. Holden smiled. If Parrish's reportorial skills were anywhere close to his abilities to describe the human face, Parrish was good.

Holden pushed up as the Ford Crown Victoria drove on along the well-paved main roadway that led both into and out of the fairgrounds. With the base commander away, odds for success, if anything, would be improved.

On his feet again, he began uncoiling more rope. His breath steamed as he worked, and when he looked to the east he could see the sun just winking full over the horizon. He had to work more rapidly.

Rose Shepherd's rope was all but played out. She shot a quick glance at the lensatic compass she'd shifted into

position around her neck on its lanyard when she'd begun laying the rope. She was still on course and the
landmark she worked toward—a water tower—was still
due east. As she started the last dozen feet she heard a
rustling sound in the pine woods near her and reached
for the Detonics Servicemaster .45, thumbing back the
hammer as she dropped flat into the pine straw.

But she was greeted by a wave and a shrug from
Mitch Diamond. As he walked toward her from the
trees with the hook-ended aircraft cable in his left hand
and a Mini-14 in the right, she rolled over onto her
butt. With the muzzle of the .45 pointed into the
ground between her legs, she interposed the thumb of
her left hand between the hammer and the rear of the
slide, gently lowering the hammer to full rest.

She stood, reholstered the .45, then shook the rest of
the ski rope out of the day pack.

David Holden had fed nearly all the rope out of his
pack.

"David!"

He wheeled toward the source of the rasped feminine
whisper, seeing little Patsy Alfredi coming toward him
around a bracken edged by a copse of wild-growing,
out-of-season honeysuckle. In one hand Patsy carried
an AR-15 by the pistol grip, but with the other she led a
length of cable terminating in a sturdy locking hook.
Holden shot her a grin and holstered the Desert Eagle,
then dropped to his knees and set to weaving a sturdy
Boy Scout square knot into the butt of the rope.

Rose Shepherd followed Mitch Diamond down the
hard-packed red clay of the embankment and, after
him, jumped the ditch beside the service road onto the
hard-packed gravel, the small stones crunching under

her boots as she picked up the pace, running. One of the wreckers was already hitched up to the cable, David standing beside it, martialing the rest of the first assault group around him.

The red-and-white painted wreckers were enormous, the type used on interstate highways to tow crippled eighteen-wheelers. David shouted some last-minute orders, looked over toward her as she stood beside Mitch while he hooked up to the second wrecker. He gave her a thumbs-up and she gave one back. Each of the wreckers, Mitch had told her as they'd run back following the course of the cable, was powered by a 400-cubic-inch Cummings diesel with thirteen-speed transmission in the power train.

Mitch shouted to the two drivers who stood beside their vehicles, the engines already rumbling loudly, reassuringly. "Okay. Now remember, just like you're pullin' a trashed load of eggs that ain't broken yet, right?"

Both drivers—one of them was a woman of about Rose's age—nodded back and clambered aboard. "And listen for that signal." He called to David, "We're ready!"

David took up a hand radio set from his belt. As she moved toward him—he was already leading the first assault group toward the front gates—she could pick up part of his transmission: ". . . signal. I repeat, attack on my signal. Group One leader, Out."

She fell in step beside him, but already the men and women Patriots were into a jog trot, the sounds of rifle bolts being worked, the rattle of equipment, more sounds of crunching gravel. The sun was fully up over the horizon, peering sideways at her as she looked toward the water tower, but the morning was still gray and the air was damp. Rose Shepherd pulled the industrial zipper of the M-65 field jacket she wore up higher, the collar closer around her throat.

Every man and woman wore the shoulder brassard of the Patriots. It was nothing more elaborate than an American flag.

Chapter Three

"**T**his is Group One leader to all units. Now. I say again, now. Out."

David Holden pouched the radio and looked at Rose Shepherd for the briefest instant. "Move out!" He was up, moving out of the tree cover, jumping across the lip of the ditch flanking the main-access road, his M-16 at high port in his fists. The second element of the Group One came along the opposite side of the road. Holden stayed to one side so there would be easy access into the ditch, their only possible cover, should there be a heavy volume of fire.

Guards stationed at the main gate—four of them—turned toward them, raising their weapons to open fire. David Holden shouted, "Grenades!" Then he dodged left, letting the grenadier just behind pass him, drop to one knee, and open fire with the Hawk MM-1 grenade launcher. As the grenadier fired his first round, Holden brought his rifle to his shoulder, thumbing the safety tumbler to the auto position, firing a burst toward the guards, then another and another, bringing one man down in the instant before the first of the grenades exploded.

One man and a chunk of the outer gate blew skyward. Three more grenades, the remaining two men were down, the outer gate structure collapsed. Gunfire and some small explosions—likely more grenades—could be heard from the far rear of the camp perimeter. Assault Group Two, Holden thought mechanically. Holden snatched up his belt radio. "This is Group One leader to trucks. Do it now. I say again, do it now! Out!"

They reached the remains of the main-gate guard station. On either side of them, the fence was beginning to vibrate, rattle. Gunfire emanated from one of the guard barracks just beyond the interior gate, men standing on the porch in various stages of undress, firing M-16s, others firing from cover by the building walls. The range worked as much against the guards as it did Holden's Patriot personnel, almost an even two hundred yards. Holden's element and the second element on the other side of the road took cover in the ditch.

"Hit that barracks!" Holden shouted, shouldering his M-16 and firing. At the distance his best hope was effect, not accuracy with the puny 5.56mm ball rounds, not in the hands of people, some of whom had never had formal marksmanship training beyond familiarization and using guns designed for intense combat-range firepower and not for long-range man-stopping. For every ex-cop or Vietnam veteran in the Metro Patriot cell, there were three or four people who'd never picked up a gun that was anything more than a deer rifle. "Full auto. Sweep that porch!"

The grenadiers from both units fired, the first grenade falling short, the Hawk MM-1's maximum effective range falling well over two hundred meters, with the high-explosive round each of the twelve-shot revolving cylinder launchers had loaded. Operator error. But they tore a crater into the far right side of the road that ran between the guard barracks. The enemy gunfire reduced in volume for a few seconds as the second grenadier's round impacted. The second grenadier, closer, had better luck, a portion of the blast bathing the barracks porch in debris and fragments, downing three of the Presidential Strike Force personnel.

The chain link was rattling louder now, the metal almost singing, the verticals along the fence's length pulsating violently. "Grenadiers! Concentrate on both barracks—the roofs!"

No response was necessary. "Schuler and Browne—cover the grenadiers. Rest of both teams—follow me!" And David Holden was up, Rosie suddenly beside him again as he streaked toward the demolished front gates. Gunfire from the barracks to his left, bullet impacts plowing ragged furrows into the dirt twenty-five yards ahead of him. Holden fired back. Useless, he knew, at the range, but it beat just letting them shoot at him.

Through the outer gate, to the inner gate, the Patriots fanning out on either side of him. And then there was a tearing sound, loud as thunder, and Holden glanced back. The fence on both sides of the outer gate was tearing away, the chain link sheering from the pipelike verticals, the bindings snapped, needle-sized pieces of wire spraying everywhere, pinging off the bodies of vehicles parked just inside the compound perimeter.

As the walls of the fence collapsed outward, there was a flare fired from the woods beyond.

Holden shouted to Rosie, "Stick with me!" And he angled left toward the nearer of the two barracks buildings. A grenade fired by his men just outside the perimeter struck the barracks roofs. An explosion, the window glass spraying outward. Holden shifted his rifle to his left hand, tearing one of the fragmentation grenades from his web gear, ducking low as he shouted to Rosie, "Cover me!" and running for the nearest barracks wall.

He could hear the rattle of Rosie's M-16 behind him as he angled farther left, gunfire from behind the porch furrowing the ground near his combat-booted feet as he ran. But the sounds of Rosie's covering fire were suddenly drowned out beneath shouts and gunfire. Holden looked toward the fallen fence sections. The bulk of the Patriot force—Patriot cell members from communities surrounding Metro, some as far off as· a hundred and fifty miles—were storming the compound through the gaps in the fence. He was twenty yards from the nearest barracks wall now, and he hauled his right arm back and lobbed the grenade toward the nearest of the blown-out windows, reached to his web gear as the first grenade was still in flight, tearing free a second, flipping it after the first. He threw himself down as the first grenade—he'd known it was a miss when he hurled it—hit the barracks wall, exploding. Spearpoint fragments of wood rained down around him. The second grenade exploded, the hollowness of the sound convincing him he'd gotten it through the window and into the barracks building itself.

He pushed up to his feet, other Patriots forming up around him now. "Scatter!" He ran for the front porch, another grenade fired from beyond the perimeter exploding off the roof, debris raining down around him, his left hand and forearm up to cover his face and head, the M-16 spitting from his right hand as he neared the porch.

A Presidential Strike Force trooper raised up from the porch floor, the left side of his face bloodied, his M-16 firing. Holden dodged left, firing back, bullets from Holden's rifle tearing across the porch railing, wood chips flying, the PSF-er still firing.

Holden dropped, rolled, the ground beside him exploding with multiple projectile impacts. He came up to his knees, firing out the M-16, putting the PSF-er down, ramming a fresh magazine up the well as he dropped the spent one. Rosie was at the porch steps, firing her M-16 through the shot-out windows. Holden grabbed for a grenade, tore it free, freeing the pin from the spoon, at the same time shouting to Rosie, "Watch it!" He flipped the grenade up and through the window, then ran for the porch.

The concussion slapped at him, pitching him forward but not enough to lose his balance.

Presidential Strike Force personnel, some in full uniform and battle gear, others in pieces of uniforms only, pistol belts and web gear slung from shoulders, rifles in hand, stormed along the main road between the two multilevel barracks structures, trying to get away. The force stopped, exchanging shots with the advancing phalanx of Patriot volunteers, then breaking up, a moment's defiant stand turned into a riot.

Running. Shifting the M-16 to his left hand. Drawing the Desert Eagle. Holden headed for the porch. A fleeing PSF-er from the roadway streaked past him, turned, fired a burst from his M-16. Holden dropped, rolled, fired the M-16 and Desert Eagle simultaneously, two rounds from the pistol and a half dozen from the rifle spraying into the man.

Holden was up, on his feet. He reached the porch rail, jumped up and vaulted over, coming down beside a PSF-er, the man raising a Beretta M-9 in his right fist toward Holden's face. The guns in Holden's hands discharged as he stepped back, the Colt assault rifle shot out now, the magazine only a twenty-rounder. The Desert Eagle was still loaded with a half-filled magazine in his right hand. There was a fleeting impression of the PSF trooper's left eye and ear seeming to disintegrate. Holden wheeled toward a man running from the barracks door, an M-16 in each of the man's hands.

Holden and Rosie Shepherd fired simultaneously, the man's body sprawling back through the open doorway. Holden dropped the empty M-16 to his side on its sling, shifted the Desert Eagle to his left fist, snatched a grenade from his webbing and snapped it through the opening just beyond the body, the dead man's M-16s firing into the barracks ceiling. "Get outta here, Rosie!" Holden dove over the porch rail, hit the ground in a roll, the grenade exploding, a shower of wood splinters and glass shards engulfing him, his hands and arms over his face and neck.

As the impacts stopped, he was up. Rosie shouted, "Another one!" Holden threw himself down, this time nearer to the porch, out of the far left corner of his peripheral vision seeing a blur of movement just as he ducked, Rosie bowling the grenade through the open doorway, flipping the railing on the far side of the porch, and gone from sight.

Holden hit the dirt, the explosion rising and falling, more debris raining down around him. As he stood up he could feel dirt and glass and wood falling from his back. The Desert Eagle was still in his left fist and he drew the larger of his two Beretta pistols with his right, hitting the porch steps, firing both pistols through the doorway, then dropping to the base of the steps. "Anybody alive in there, give it up!"

Before an answer came, there was chatter from his radio and Holden safed the Desert Eagle .44 and stuffed it inside his pistol belt. He took up the radio. "David— you reading me?"

It was Luther Steel, leading the second element. In times of crisis, Steel himself was excellent but his radio procedures went by the board. "I'm reading you, Luther."

"We're up to the interior fences. We're checking for mines, but it doesn't look like there are any. We should get started emptying out the compound in about five. Maybe four hundred people. God, they look like they've been starved and—you wouldn't believe it, that

Americans could be treated like this by other Americans!"

"I believe it. If you can spare a dozen guys, start them forward to meet up with us by the barracks flanking the road. About forty PSF-ers should be coming your way. Have your guys watch out."

"Roger on that. Sending Tom and Randy with ten men. Bill's staying with me. He's got more experience with explosives. I've got a perimeter defense by the prison fence. Steel, Out."

Holden nodded, as if ex-FBI agent Luther Steel could somehow see him, then punched the push-to-talk button and said, "All units, this is Holden. As LeFleur and Blumenthal bring their people up, consolidate on both barracks. Tennessee and South Carolina Patriot units—keep to both sides of the main road as you move to your preassigned defensive positions. Remember, the bad guys have airpower available to them and we have to be fast. Holden, Out."

Rosie was beside him at the base of the steps, a dozen Patriots, most of them Metro people, flanking the porch on both sides. "Surrender inside or we're coming in—and we'll bring the building down around your ears if we've got to."

"Wait," someone from inside shouted. "We're coming out! Don't shoot! Don't hurt us."

David Holden looked away in disgust.

Chapter Four

*T*homas Ashbrooke's coffee mug was empty. He set it down to light a cigarette, the *Ruth II* rolling gently in the swells, her sails rigid in the wind. He knew enough about sailing to know that the man on watch in the cockpit was good at his work. They'd set sail under wind and diesel power from Nassau on the evening tide, their destination a stretch of beach somewhere in the Keys with the unlikely name of Iceman's Pain, supposedly desolate except for the occasional drug smugglers who brought their kilos of coke ashore there.

There was no coke aboard the *Ruth II*, but a cargo just as dangerous if they were caught. Beside Ashbrooke where he sat nested into the prow was a waterproof satchel, protected within it a Heckler & Koch MP5-K submachine gun and three spare magazines. It was part of the cargo: MP5-Ks, the full-sized integral suppressor MP5-SD3s, G-3s with integral under-barrel grenade launchers and Hirtenberg mil-spec ammo in 9mm Parabellum and 7.62mm NATO, along with a supply of high-explosive grenades for the launchers and spare magazines for the guns themselves.

His friends in the Mossad, one of them old enough to remember when the organization's full name—Mossad Aliya Bet, or *Going Up*—had been used, had explained it to him thusly: "Times were, Tom, when our nation struggled more than it does today, but just to survive. You didn't fail our people then, when if we didn't have guns there would have been a slaughter worse than the Holocaust under the Nazis. In the decades since, the Prime Minister told me to tell you, the American people have stuck by Israel. We won't fail your people now. But none of the matériel will be Israeli in origin. These are the very best." And then Ruben had smiled. "With the exception of the stuff we make, of course."

The *Ruth II* carried enough equipment for a commando unit of modest strength, that was all. But anything would help the freedom fighters in America who struggled under the heel of Roman Makowski, murderer of the President, usurper of his office, defiler of liberty. The very thought of this demagogue-turned-dictator turned Tom Ashbrooke's stomach.

But the *Ruth II* 's deck beneath him felt marvelously good. He inhaled on his cigarette. Smuggling had been his life until the drug thing took over and he'd killed Arturo Nunez and scuttled Nunez's ship, the *Santiago,* off the coast of West Palm Beach in a storm, after having followed Nunez across the Atlantic for the sole purpose of destroying a man who had betrayed him and a cargo that betrayed humanity.

· Those were his younger, wilder days. He would have liked to have thought of them as idealistic days, but he'd always been motivated by profit. Diane, his wife of these many years, had told him, "It's a testament to your character, Tom, that no one ever even asked why you got out of the business when it turned to drugs." Either that or they'd heard about Nunez and knew better than to bring it up.

He shifted his shoulders under the harness of the Galco holster with the SIG-Sauer P-226 in it, snapping the cigarette butt overboard, careful of the wind. He smoked rarely and he never bothered with filters, so there was no synthetic junk to remain immune to bio-degradation. He wasn't polluting the sea that had carried him so often.

Giving and paying back. It was like an amendment to the Golden Rule, or should have been. Regardless of what the payback was. The husband of his dead daughter, Elizabeth, was into the payback business these days. David Holden was the leader of the growing American revolution. If he lived long enough to succeed, David's birthday might one day be celebrated like that of Washington. If—

"What are you thinking about, Tom?"

Tom Ashbrooke turned his head toward the sound of the voice. Rachel, the daughter of his benefactor (the father owned the *Ruth II*), was pretty enough to— He smiled at his own thoughts. "I'm thinking how stupid I am to enjoy doing this sort of thing again, smuggling."

She laughed a nice, healthy woman's laugh and sat down beside him. "Give me a cigarette."

He lit one for her, inhaled, passed it to her.

"Thank you. How can you smoke these things without filters?" She was picking tobacco from her lower lip with her fingernail.

"Not wearing lipstick for the tobacco to stick to helps." Ashbrooke smiled.

"What were you thinking about, with your smuggling, you know?"

Ashbrooke didn't quite know but said what he was thinking. "I never thought it would be necessary to smuggle weapons into the United States to arm free men against a usurper."

"What is a *usurper*? I don't know the word, Tom."

Her honey-brown hair caught in the wind and she brushed it back from her face with the back of her left hand. He watched the smoke from her cigarette rise for an instant, then be whisked away. "A usurper is a thief of power, Rachel. That's all he is, no matter what he pretends to be or what he calls himself. A usurper is a Roman Makowski."

"I am curious." She smiled.

"A woman's being curious isn't a novelty at my age, Rachel," Ashbrooke told her, shifting slightly in his seat. He was getting stiff, sitting next to this marvelously pretty girl, but in his legs rather than someplace more obvious; and that was a horrible reminder to him that he was easily old enough to be her father.

"Would you kill this dictator, this Roman Makowski?"

He didn't have to think about the answer. "In a second."

Chapter Five

*T*he wreckers were already on the move, disappearing into garages in suburban Metro. Rose Shepherd absently wondered if they'd passed the eighteen-wheelers on the road leading into the fairgrounds compound from the interstate.

These new trucks were filling rapidly with human cargo—the prisoners—men, women, and some few children who had been held here without arraignment, without trial, without consultation with an attorney, for the most part on gun charges, many of these charges trumped up merely as an excuse to incarcerate a person deemed actually or potentially politically dangerous. In some cases, as with Lem Parrish's engineer from the radio station, as a warning to some other, more powerful person, to watch what he said lest the same thing happen to him.

She hadn't ever met Lem's engineer and had no idea which face in the throng of humanity milling past her was his, other than that the face would be black. But there were many blacks here as well as whites, Hispanics, some few Asians also.

"All right—this one's full. The people have to breathe!" Rose shouted to the loading crew of the semitrailer truck nearest her, the trailer filled to capacity where the people would have to sit in rows, some back-to-back, some facing one another, for the journey awaiting them. Each truckload was given a short recruitment message before leaving, the purpose to swell the ranks of the Metro Patriots. Those who elected to join would be transferred to a different truck; the others would stay aboard the one where they already were, their destinations small towns and farms in the Carolinas and Alabama, where they would be helped until they could blend into society under a new identity. Already the Metro cell in Miami was working on the mass production of Social Security cards and driver's licenses, but the work was slow in order to get it right and there was a shortage of blanks and properly marked clear plastic sealers for the licenses.

Rose Shepherd mounted the rear of the trailer, the arm of one of the male Patriots from South Carolina extended to her. She didn't need help, was probably more agile and fit than he was, but she never denied a man the opportunity to treat her like a lady, regardless of the circumstances. "Thanks, friend." She nodded, standing to her full height then at the rear of the trailer in the doorframe. "All right. Give me your attention, please. This'll only take a minute. I have an announcement." The whir of muted conversation began to subside. "And afterward I'll take a minute to answer a couple of questions. My name is Rose Shepherd. If you mail a lot of letters, you've probably seen my picture on the wall."

There was some laughter.

Rose cleared her throat, her palms sweating inside her gloves. She hated giving speeches. "If you don't know who we are yet or haven't noticed the American-flag patches on our shoulders, well, we're the Patriots, the guys everybody in the media dumps on. But we're only some of the Patriots. There are thousands more like us all across the United States, and our numbers are growing almost by the hour. Ever since FBI Director Rudolph Cerillia's deathbed-statement videotape was broadcast, naming Roman Makowski as the man behind the murder of the real President, a lot of people have started waking up.

"Some of you may wonder," Rose Shepherd continued, "what kind of political program we're for. Well, we're for the Constitution—not a heck of a lot more and not a damn sight less. We want Roman Makowski impeached and tried for murder. We want the legitimate government—what's left of it—to beat the crap out of the Front for the Liberation of North America and imprison or deport every FLNA-er nobody's had a chance to kill yet. And then we want things to go pretty much back to the way they were—but not quite.

"We're tired," Rose said, "of innocent citizens getting the blame for every half-assed criminal who decides to shoot up somebody, when the prisons are overcrowded, the death penalty almost never gets handed out, the courts are a revolving door, and most serious felonies never result in an arrest and those that do rarely get a conviction but those that do are almost never full sentence. So they pass more laws that get down on innocent people because innocent, law-abiding people obey the laws and the scumbag criminals don't, so it's a lot easier to make laws that hassle the good guys.

"I guess," she added, "we want America to go back to being America, for everybody—white, black, or any other color, religion, no religion, or in between. Maybe we needed this to happen to wake us all up. And God help us if we don't win. Because we're paying a big price, and if we blow this, everybody loses forever.

"I guess"—Rose smiled, realizing suddenly how silly she must look in her black BDUs and her weapons and her hair bound up in a black bandana and cammie stick rubbed on her cheeks and forehead—"I guess this is a recuiting speech. Pep talk to get some of you to sign up. I never tried a pitch like this before. I was a cop, not a vacuum-cleaner saleslady." There was some weak laughter. "But we need men and women as fighters, as support personnel for everything you can imagine an army might need. The pay just isn't. The fringe benefits are cold showers and the ground under you instead of a mattress and a box spring. The hours really suck too." She smiled. "But there's plenty to do and so far we've been able to keep everybody in two or three squares a day, and sometimes the food's even hot.

"So," she concluded. "Any questions?"

A teenage girl from the middle of the trailer stood up. Her face was dirty, her hair straggly and needing a brushing, and her blue jeans ripped, which might have been the style rather than from wear, but Rose didn't think so. "Ma'am?"

"Yes?"

"How old you have to be to join up in the Patriots?" Some woman beside her, probably her mother, was pulling at her pants leg, to get her to sit down.

"Old enough"—Rosie grinned—"old enough to risk your life so you can have a future. That's how old."

The girl stepped over another woman to get away from the woman tugging at her. "I'm signin' up."

Rose looked at the still-seated woman who'd been tugging at the girl's pants leg, then said to the girl, "If you can work it out with your family—because we don't want to split up families or cause trouble between people—but if you can, see me outside. Anybody else have a question?"

A man stood up. He wore what was left of a gray business suit—just the vest and dirty slacks—and looked about Rose's own age, was skinny, needed a shave. He asked, "What about all the stories we hear? That the Patriots are just a bunch of gun nuts?"

There was some booing, some shouting him down. Rose outstretched both hands, saying, "Hey! Give the man the chance to talk!"

"Well," he said more emphatically, "what about it?"

Rose Shepherd answered, "I guess, as a group, if you could say the Patriots have a common belief besides a faith in the idea of America, the Constitution, self-government, freedom, you could say that we all kind of figure that freedom means people have to be responsible for staying free, and people have the right to choose—"

"But you run around with military weapons and—hell, just look at you, a woman running around dressed up like she's in some kinda damn war movie—"

"Hey," she snapped. "I let you ask your question, let me answer it. And this isn't a damn movie but sure as hell is war. Guns are tools, just like anything else. You pick up a spoon and you eat your soup with it—or you can stab somebody in the eyeball with it—the spoon's still a spoon. You can use a gun to defend your home, your country, your freedom, any kind of gun you choose, or you can use a gun to kill innocent people. But you're using it, the thing, the gun or the spoon or a car or whatever—it doesn't do anything. You use it because you have the ability to choose, because you're a person, and guns and spoons and stuff don't have any choices to make, because they're just things, not people, so they can't do anything on their own at all. They aren't good, they aren't bad, they're just there, waiting for somebody to use them for a good purpose or a bad purpose.

"People have the right to choose," she told him, told all of them, feeling her blood pressure rising, her cheeks flushing. "That's what this whole thing is about. Nobody has the right to tell me what I can or can't do, can or can't own, can or can't say, can or can't think, unless what I'm doing is hurting other people. If I start using violence first, I'm wrong. But if somebody starts using violence against me and I use violence back to defend myself or my rights or my country or my family, I've got the right to use as much violence as necessary to keep that guy from being violent against me.

"I don't know what they threw you into this camp for, but a lot of the people here were illegally imprisoned because of supposed gun crimes—they just happened to own something some idiot lawmaker decided to make illegal and whammo! Instant crook! Don't even need to add water or use a microwave oven. Well, bullshit! If I wanna own a damn tank or grow daisies on the living room rug or hang family photos on the roof or take a bath in chocolate sauce, and I don't hurt somebody, don't try to intimidate somebody, don't try to make somebody else do it with me, but just enjoy myself, who gave some half-assed hypocrite the right to tell me I can't? Huh? Who has the right to tell me or you or anybody else how to live their life, huh? The bad guys came and got you and everybody else in this truck, threw you all into a damn outdoor pen, kept you here without reading you the friggin' Miranda card, letting you see a lawyer, having formal charges pressed against you, any of that.

"They kept you here at gunpoint. They had the guns, you didn't. They started the violence, you didn't. We released you guys because they held you prisoner. We took prisoners, disarmed them, we're interrogating them and just because we don't have a place to lock 'em up, we're not killing 'em, we're lettin' them go. We believe in human rights and they don't. So maybe that's why I'm dressed up in black battle gear instead of a pink party dress. Because they threw the party," she hissed, "and they made up the invitation list and only slimeballs got asked. So me and a whole bunch of people like me—I made up my own dress code and came along to the party anyway. And if somebody doesn't like it, that's his lookout, not mine. Because the party's on my property. I'm payin' for it and I'm gonna be stuck cleanin' up after it's all over, but what I think, what I want, what I am, that doesn't matter, because all they care about is themselves. And that's cool, but not at my expense. So they're just shit outta luck.''

She shut up.

The men and women in the truck trailer started to stand up, applaud, some of them whistling, some of them shouting.

Rose Shepherd was never so embarrassed in her life.

Chapter Six

*T*he train had been slowing for the past ten or twelve minutes and finally stopped. All the while, as much as he could in the hot, stench-heavy air, Lieutenant Wood worked to loosen the muscles in his legs and back and stomach. It was necessary to stop periodically, just try to breathe by getting his face close to the bars, waiting for the vagrant, fleeting wash of cool, clean air.

"Be ready, Wood," the marine colonel, Young, told him.

"Yes, sir."

Through the bars, in the fresh dawn light outside, he could see the guards, all of them in the starched cammie fatigues of the Presidential Strike Force, all of them with M-16s, except for one officer who had what looked from the distance like two M-9 Berettas on his pistol belt and was trying to come off like some kind of war hero, Wood surmised.

Barnabas Wood stood there at the center of the car on the farthest end from the doors, beside the bars where he would try to get his fresh air. The air was staler now, the train fully stopped, the doors to some of the boxcars already opening. A maximum of three cars were opened up at once, and since the doors to the car in which he was confined weren't opening yet, he realized there was a wait in store.

A young air force lieutenant, about Wood's own age, started talking animatedly. "Hey, look! Look there! Shit!"

Wood crossed the boxcar floor, stepping over or around officers too weak to stand, too tired to be curious. There was a growing knot, however, of those who could still move around, who were still interested in whatever marvelous thing the air force lieutenant saw.

And it was at once marvelous—just the sight of a woman—and also sickening. About three dozen of them, some in partially assembled dress uniforms—skirts and blouses, an open uniform jacket, one of them shoeless—and others in fatigues. Every branch seemed to be represented, and they looked as dirty and disheveled as the men of the boxcar in which he rode.

He heard loud talking and looked toward the knot of PSF personnel standing at the boxcar doors. Hero with the two Berettas—a captain—was ordering, "Open up the fuckin' car. We're taking too damn long. Be ready to hose 'em all down and the inside of the car."

There were fire hoses being brought forward from a military fire truck, and Wood noticed for the first time that there were three hydrants near the siding.

The doors to the boxcar were thrown open and a noncom shouted, "All right, gentlemen—off your asses and outta the car, else you get washed out with the car instead of out here. Suit yourselves."

Wood looked at Colonel Young. At least three of the men were so weak that Colonel Young was already giving orders: "Let's get everybody up and outta here. Now. Look sharp. Gotta let those women see us out there still looking like officers."

There were grunted "Yes sirs" and nods, and men that Wood wouldn't have thought were still able started to their knees, then to their feet.

The colonel looked at him. "You ready, Lieutenant?"

"Yes, sir."

"I'd say past those fire hydrants and over that embankment. Wish to God I knew what was on the other side."

"That's what I was planning, sir. When I bring help, I'll tell you what's on the other side."

The field-grade marine officer outstretched his hand quickly. Wood took it. "Good luck, Lieutenant. You'll make it. I've got a feeling. You'll make it." And the colonel announced to the man nearest him, "He's going —pass it on."

Wood started toward the opening, catching up one of the weaker men, a naval ensign, helping him to walk. There was no platform or ramp. To get off the car, you jumped.

At a signal from the colonel, the men of the boxcar would jump the guards and he, Barnabas Wood, would run.

Some men would die, he knew.

Maybe it would have been better to jump the guards from the height of the car, while the boxcar was being unloaded of the men aboard. But that was the marine colonel's decision.

Wood eased the young ensign down, then eased down himself, trying to look weaker than he felt and guarding against turning an ankle while exiting the car and blowing the whole thing.

"Hurry it up, Lieutenant," the Presidential Strike Force corporal with the M-16 snarled.

"Fuck off, soldier," Wood snarled back, feeling dizzy with the freshness of the air.

The corporal started to buttstroke him, but Wood backed away and a group of other officers from the boxcar interposed themselves between Wood and the corporal.

Wood helped the ensign down, started walking him

away from the boxcar. There was no siding here, just gravel and dirt and a sea of tracks surrounding them as far as he could see, front and back. There had been more tracks on the far side of the car. But maybe two hundred yards off, there was a low rise and a drop. He didn't know what lay beyond it, could see nothing that would give him the slightest clue.

He started regulating his breathing, out of the corner of his eyes alternating between watching the PSF troopers as they brought up the fire hoses and the female officers on the ground several cars ahead.

"Hey, Navy!" one of the marine officers from Wood's boxcar shouted. And a female naval officer—there was no sign of her rank that Wood could see—turned around, shot him a feeble smile. "How about a drink?"

"I outrank you, sonny." She laughed.

"Doesn't bother me if it doesn't bother you—ma'am."

A few of the women and some of the men laughed.

Hero with the two pistols at his hips shouted, "Knock off the chatter, assholes, or we see how much power these fire hoses really got, huh?"

The laughter ended abruptly.

The first hose started, two more still being connected to hydrants, three PSF troopers wrestling it into position in front of one of the other boxcars, spraying the water across the boxcar floor.

Sure, Wood thought, the hose would clean away some of the filth, but the dampness would make the occupants even sicker. Who were the Presidential Strike Force people kidding? Or did they even care at all?

Did they want the men and women aboard this train —other trains like it?—to die of "natural causes" rather than have to explain away bodies with bullet holes at the backs of the heads? At the Point, his military history had included studying the Katyn Forest Massacre, the slaughter of the Polish officer corps during World War Two. Both the Nazis and the Russians had gone to great lengths to show their innocence of the atrocity, but in the final analysis, even though the Poles had been shot with German bullets, their hands had been tied with Russian ropes. The German ammunition and the weapons to fire it had come from a shipment of arms sent by Hitler to Stalin before Hitler had attacked his onetime ally. The Russians had been planning ahead for the absorption of Poland after the war.

Perhaps these Presidential Strike Force personnel, and the dicatator whom they served, had learned from experience and were striving for subtlety.

Barnabas Wood caught Colonel Young's eye. The colonel nodded so slightly that the gesture was imperceptible unless looked for.

Wood shook out his shoulders and his legs, bent over slightly to loosen his stomach muscles, inhaling the fresh air again.

This time the dizziness was less a bother.

His gaze drifted with as much studied casualness as he could muster—he'd never been much for amateur dramatics—toward the little knoll over which he must run to have even the slightest chance of escape before the weapons in the hands of the PSF troopers struck him down.

He heard a shout, a burst of assault-rifle fire, a scream, and wheeled toward the women several cars ahead. What he saw looked like a small riot, the female officers attacking the PSF personnel, a girl with brilliant red hair, her uniform skirt plastered against her up above her thighs, barefoot, shoes in her hands, running as if the devil were chasing her toward the knoll.

Wood shouted, "Now!"

He threw himself into a dead run, straight-arming the

trooper nearest him with a locked elbow behind the palm he shoved against the man's face.

Gunfire. Shouts.

Wood ran for the knoll, the redhead just ahead of him. She was fast for a woman. "Hell," Wood gasped, sucking air. She would have been fast for a man, and barefoot too.

Bullets furrowed the ground near his feet.

He kept running.

More gunfire from behind him.

He couldn't look back.

And he forgot the gunfire, the men who would be chasing after him. He forgot it all when he looked again at the red-haired girl, air force, from the blue color of her skirt, elbows cocked, shoes in her hands, running dead out for the knoll.

He forgot everything else, everything else but the race between them to reach the knoll.

Wood felt his nostrils twitch with dilation, lips drawing back over his teeth, neck muscles setting, stomach muscles tightening.

Run.

The redhead was fast.

How fast could she do the one hundred?

She was at the base of the knoll, gunfire tearing into the dirt just ahead of her. She dodged left but didn't really break her stride.

"Come on!" It was his voice shouting.

She fell.

"Move your ass, Airman!" Wood shouted.

The redhead was up, the ground beside her rippling under the impact of automatic-weapons fire. A burst of gunfire, then another and another tore into the ground just ahead of him. Wood dodged left, almost even with the redhead now.

Shouts from behind him. "Stop or die!"

They were admirably direct, these Presidential Strike Force personnel. He kept running.

More gunfire. Something tore at his left thigh and he fell flat to the ground. As he went down he saw the redhead reaching the summit of the knoll. She wheeled toward him. "Hey, GI, move your ass!"

Wood pushed himself up, his leg nearly buckling, lurching forward up the knoll, more gunfire all around him.

The redhead was gone, over the height of the knoll. Wood quickened his pace, his left thigh on fire with pain. Running.

The ground began sloping up ahead of him. Gunfire heavy on his right. Wood dodged left, willing the pain away.

The height of the knoll.

He looked over as he crossed it.

"Holy shit!" Wood gasped.

The redhead was standing a few feet below him, looking at him almost pleadingly. "What'll we do? You got a plan?"

"Didn't you have a plan?"

"Run like hell was the plan."

"Same plan. Now we swim like hell."

A canal of some sort. It looked deep. He hoped it was, because they would run out of ground in two long strides and the voices of the PSF personnel behind them were getting louder.

Wood grabbed the redhead's right hand in his left and started to run again, about two strides all his leg had left, he thought.

They jumped, feet first, the canal looking suddenly so much farther below them, so much shallower, dirtier.

They impacted simultaneously and for a split second he wondered if they could do other things simultaneously and he was ashamed of the thought because of his girl and because of this girl. She was an officer in the United States armed forces, just like him.

Under the water.

He hadn't taken a deep enough breath.

He lost her hand.

His leg screamed at him with pain.

Wood was going down.

The redhead's hands were in his hair and his head hurt as she hauled him up. "You all right?" she sputtered.

Wood nodded, looking around to orient himself. The knoll was behind and above them. "This way!" He coughed.

He swam for it, dragging his left leg, the muscles there knotting up. He hadn't thought to ask if she could swim but assumed she could, since she'd pulled him up. The opposite bank of the canal was steep, gouged red clay with embedded gravel and some broken bottles.

He reached out, just missing a shard of glass, pulling himself out, the redhead right beside him, shots glancing off the surface of the canal, off the embankment along which they moved.

Wood was running again. He didn't know how he was making his left leg move. He slipped, caught himself, the redhead helping him up. He noticed her shoes in the side pockets of her skirt. They were medium-heeled shoes, not the sensible kind with flat soles.

He was running again.

Along the embankment the redhead was shouting to him, "How about here?"

He nodded agreement, not knowing to what, the pain in his leg making him light-headed.

But he started after her, skidding back a foot for every two feet he climbed up a defile, some sort of naturally formed runoff channel, he guessed.

Gunfire tore into the ground on either side of them.

As he looked up, the redhead slipping, his right hand going to her butt, pushing her up, he saw her left forearm, some kind of wound there with a lot of bright red blood. "Watch the hands!" the redhead shrieked.

The height of the embankment.

There were vehicles everywhere. Just a regular parking lot. "Come on, Red, let's find a car with keys in it!" He was hoping. He was hoping that even in these days southerners would be southerners and leave their cars unlocked and the keys in the ignition or inside the ashtray.

Red lurched along ahead of him, holding her left forearm just below the elbow with her right hand. He fell to his knees, shouted to her, "Get outta here. Get help!"

"Nuts!" She ran back for him, dropping to a crouch beside him, hauling his left arm over and across her shoulders, helping him to stand.

"Air force people don't take orders?"

"What rank are you?"

"Second lieutenant."

"Date of commission?"

He started to answer her, but gunfire tore across the parking-lot surface and he looked back. "Run!" He limped beside her, the nearest vehicle a Chevy pickup truck. He could see that the doors were locked.

"This way!" He hobbled past the truck, swinging himself along by its hood.

There was a British racing green Jaguar XJ-6. Red wrenched at the door handle on the driver's side. It opened.

She left him to lean against the roof as she dropped behind the wheel. "Where are the damn keys?" She had the ashtray open.

"Under the floor mat. Try under the floor mat!"

She bent, curled the rattan mat back. "Got 'em!"

Wood looked behind them, Presidential Strike Force personnel in sopping-wet BDUs were running along the embankment.

The Jaguar's engine roared to life. He slid up onto the hood, rolled over, crashed down, dragged himself to the passenger door. It shot open, nearly hitting him in the face. "Watch it, Red!"

Wood climbed inside, the Jaguar starting into motion as soon as he was half into the passenger bucket. He dragged the door closed after him as the Jaguar shot ahead.

"Hang on, GI, I used to park cars in Chicago summers when I was in college!"

He started to wonder what that meant but found out as she stomped the brake, nearly sent him through the windshield, then started a fast, straight-as-an-arrow reverse, skidding, letting the rear end fishtail right, hauling the front end into a U-turn, then stomping the gas.

A burst of assault-rifle fire skittered across the rear deck and spiderwebbed the rear window.

She told him her commission date.

It superseded his by ninety days.

Chapter Seven

*C*olonel Young called the officers, male and female, to attention.

Captain Brandon of the Presidential Strike Force stepped a few paces forward, hands resting on the butts of his holstered pistols, three dozen men with M-16 assault rifles surrounding Marine Lieutenant Colonel Young, the men and women under his *de facto* command as ranking man.

Five male and three female officers had been killed during the break—successful? He prayed that it was—made by Wood and the red-haired female air force officer. Another eight were wounded, only two seriously.

Captain Brandon cleared his throat, spoke. "The President ordered your incarcerations through Mr. Townes because he was afraid of something just like this—insurrection."

There were murmurs from the men and women ranked behind Young, and he snapped, "As you were!"

Silence.

"Thank you, Colonel. Under the circumstances, I hate giving you what amounts to good news, but a suitable location has been found for housing you more properly while your individual cases await disposition. Trucks will be arriving shortly to take you in small groups to your billetings."

"Captain—with what crimes are we being charged?" Young called out.

"Various crimes, Colonel, but you and each officer here will have his chance to vindicate himself. I assure you of that."

"What about the dead, Captain Brandon? How will they be vindicated?"

"I will remind you, Colonel, that your officers acted rashly, attacked my men without provocation, and my men merely reacted in self-defense—"

"Fuck off, Captain."

Brandon didn't seem to know what to say. Young watched him intently.

"I'll chart that remark off to the circumstances this morning. We're all on edge. To continue, you will be billeted in warehouses that have been set up for this specific purpose. Showers and hot food and fresh clothes will be made available. No shortages. Plenty for all. And processing of formal charges and consultation with military defense counsel will begin almost immediately."

"Can we, Captain, bring charges against you?" There were shouts from behind Young: right on's, damn right's, and the like. "As you were!" Young ordered again.

"That is your privilege, Colonel, but you'll find I was only following lawful orders. Now, two choices before the trucks arrive. Voluntarily bind each other's hands behind the back—"

"Fuck you!" The shout came from well back in the ranks, a woman's voice.

"As you were!" Brandon snapped. "Voluntarily, as I say," he continued, "or we'll take you off in small groups. That will take a lot longer, Colonel, but with the same result. The longer you take, the longer before your wounded reach the proper medical attention awaiting them at your billeting. What'll it be, Colonel?"

Young eyed the men surrounding them. If everyone broke and ran in every possible different direction, maybe ten of the officers held prisoner might get as far away as the knoll. What lay beyond it he had no way of telling. Everyone else would be killed.

And there were the wounded to consider.

If Wood and the red-haired female officer had escaped, or even one of them, help might already be on the way. Risking more lives would be pointless. "We'll tie ourselves, Captain. But before we do, I have your word that we are indeed on our way to a proper facility where medical attention, shower facilities, and legal counsel will be available?"

"My word as a fellow officer, sir."

Young licked his lips. "Give us the rope."

Chapter Eight

*T*he coffee tasted slightly bitter, and he wondered if it was his imagination or really the coffee. He set down the cup, lit a cigarette, and stared at Linda Effingham across the little table from him.

There was a background of chatter at the truck stop, men discussing everything from speed traps to routes around construction to President Makowski's latest Executive Orders—a hodgepodge of draconian restrictions on civil liberties, including imprisonment on "open charges" for up to ninety days.

"You're not thinking about me." Linda Effingham smiled. Her eyes, her auburn hair—she was so wonderfully lovely.

"No, I wasn't." He smiled back.

"Geoff—you've been wanting to tell me something. What is it?"

Kearney inhaled on his cigarette. "I think you know, darling." The waitress came, offered more coffee, but Linda shook her head no. When the waitress had flitted off to the next table with her Pyrex pot of inky black liquid, Geoffrey Kearney said, "You're at once right and wrong. I haven't been wanting to tell you, but I have to tell you—what it is I've been thinking of, I mean."

"You're going to leave me," she whispered, no longer

looking at him, her fingers drumming nervously on the table top.

"Yes. Or rather you're going to leave me."

"No," she whispered, her voice strained-sounding. "I love you."

"And I love you, which is exactly why you're going to leave me."

"I love you. I am not leaving you," Linda said, looking away, out the window. "We worked pretty well together, I thought."

"We worked very well together," Kearney said, trying to control his voice, staring at the disgusting-tasting excuse for coffee in the cup in front of him. He sipped at it again. Still bitter. "But that's not the point."

"What isn't?"

"Working well together or love either, for that matter. It's too dangerous for you. We're talking a full-blown revolution here and all the marvelous things that entails. War. This is a war zone, now more than it was before, and I don't like you in the middle of it."

She looked up at him and smiled. "So you mean I'd be safer if I weren't around you—"

"Exactly."

"I'd be safer in the middle of this war with somebody else instead of you, with a bunch of people—maybe my aunt who never touched a gun in her life?—with a bunch of people who don't know anything about how to protect themselves. And they could protect me."

"Dammit," Kearney hissed. "All right. Fine. You want to play spy and assassin and all the fun little games I play, then you'll learn how. Get up!"

Geoffrey Kearney stood up, threw a dollar bill on the table, grabbed up the check for the two cups of coffee, and started toward the register, saying, "Dammit" under his breath instead of slapping her.

Chapter Nine

*H*e wiggled his toes in the sand.

There had been a time when he'd wondered if he'd ever use his legs again.

The sand felt warm in contrast to the cool fall midday and when he went closer to the surf—he still used two canes but more to steady himself—and the water touched his feet, it felt warm as well.

Life was good.

Roman Makowski had totally asserted himself as dictator, was believed by almost everyone to be the architect of the President's murder—which he was, of course —and there was civil war heating to the boiling point, just ready to boil over because of some otherwise minuscule incident, but the perfect incident. There was no need to contrive it. If it didn't happen today, it would happen tomorrow or the next day.

Some one of the degenerates from among the ranks of the Presidential Strike Force would kill a child or rape a woman or defile a church and that would be the spark. There would be a new Crispus Attucks who would become history's first casualty and a new Shot Heard Round the World.

Only this time the results would be very, very different.

God was in his heaven—the perfect place for him

rather than meddling in the affairs of earth—and all was right with the world.

Dimitri Borsoi smiled.

He walked—hobbled—along the beach, in his mind preparing the wording for the soon-to-be-released declaration of cease-fire by the Front for the Liberation of North America.

Chapter Ten

*T*he Jaguar had only a quarter of a tank of gas when they stole it and the gauge was below empty by noon. With no money, smelling like human fecal material, and both with wounds hastily bandaged with strips of the red-haired girl's slip, they couldn't just pull into a gas station and say, Fill 'er up and check my oil, wouldya?

If any convenience stores remained where someone could fill up the car without paying first to have the pumps turned on, such places had to be found in the middle of nowhere, the Front for the Liberation of North America notorious for stealing gasoline, the least of the FLNA's crimes.

They abandoned the car, Wood taking the jack handle as a weapon and the red-haired girl finding one of the nondisposable versions of Thermos space blankets. With the car at the side of the interstate highway they'd entered less than a half an hour before, they waited for a break in traffic, crossed the four lanes of highway and started up the opposite embankment, Wood's leg paining him so badly that he felt faint. But he didn't want to tell that to the girl.

And the way he thought of her bothered him. He hadn't even asked her name, just started calling her Red, and even though she was obviously a quite competent officer and even outranked him on a technicality, he kept thinking of her as a girl. "Let me carry the jack handle, Jimmy."

"Jimmy?"

"Yeah—I started thinking about Jimmy Durante when I caught your profile." She positively blushed. "I mean, I didn't know what to call you and you were calling me Red, and everything, and when I was a little girl—oh, watch that rock—I saw some Jimmy Durante movies and my dad used to sing some of his songs, so anyway, he had a nose."

"Everybody's got a nose."

"Look, I don't have to call you Jimmy, but I gotta call you something!" They had reached the height of the embankment and his leg gave out, and as he started to fall she caught him a little, stumbled herself, and eased him down. Immediately a cold sweat came over him with the pain. He started moving himself back farther from the embankment with his hands and his good leg. She helped him. "If we can get over the fence, I can take a better look at that leg."

"The bullet went through, I think. Look, Red, I'll be fine here. You keep that jack handle and the blanket and—"

"And what? Go to the police? Find a military base? Get myself arrested or shot? Nuts. We've gotta find some of the Patriots."

"What?" He just stared at her.

"I mean, they're on the side of the American people, aren't they? So they've gotta be against Makowski and the goons from the Presidential Strike Force. Right? I mean, right?"

"Yeah, but—" He heard the sounds of the helicopter, grabbed her, and shook her. "Run for those trees!"

"Nuts!" And she grabbed him by the left arm and hauled him up to his feet, half helping him to walk, half dragging him west along the height of the embankment toward a stand of pines that looked to have been planted there, they were ranked so orderly.

Wood looked skyward, placed the helicopter then, and realized it was military. "Shit, they're lookin' for us, Red."

"I figured they would be. I mean, didn't you?"

And he looked at her. She had pretty green eyes. Her face was dirty, but he could still see freckles, not a lot of them, just enough to be cute. And past her, he saw the space blanket. The silver side was folded out and, the jack handle beside it, it lay in full sunlight, the silver side so reflective that only a blind man could have missed it from the air.

She must have seen his eyes and she turned around.

"Holy smokes!" He tried grabbing at her, but she slipped through his fingers and ran out to get the blanket.

"Red! No, dammit! Red!"

She was nearly up to where the folded blanket lay, reached for it. The helicopter swept over the interstate, its shadow passing over her, a voice on a PA speaker ordering, "Stand right where you are or be fired upon!"

She clutched the blanket.

She looked into the trees toward him.

He saw her lips move, couldn't tell what she said. And she smiled.

Clutching the blanket against her chest, she ran away from the trees, toward the roadway, the helicopter arcing, sweeping over her again. "Halt!" It was the same voice.

Wood pushed himself along the ground, trying to get nearer to the slope, his eyes picking her up again. She was nearly onto the roadbed.

The helicopter hovered.

"Nose" saw a glint of metal or maybe a telescopic

sight. A burst of assault-rifle fire cracked across the air over the thrumming of the rotor blades.

"Red!"

His eyes filled with tears, but he couldn't stop watching as she rolled down the embankment, her dirty white blouse all streaked red. "Red!"

Chapter Eleven

*I*t looked too shallow a draft. Rachel, beside him in the prow of the *Ruth II*, must have read his thoughts. "There's a channel. The man at the helm used to be a drug smuggler. He's a thoroughly disreputable man, but he likes our money. When he lost his leg—"

"You don't have to—"

"They cut it off with a chain saw," Rachel continued, calm-sounding, like the lapping of the water against the hull of the *Ruth II*. "But he couldn't work anymore and he was so angry at his old business associates—he almost bled to death and, of course, he's crippled for life —he just stopped doing that. He's a good man for what he does. He knows this channel like the back of his hand."

"There was a study done some years back." Ashbrooke smiled, his eyes never leaving the beach. It was gray-purple in shadow there, light still on the water but the beach and the rock-strewn area beyond it darkening quickly with the setting sun. "They found out that most people couldn't tell the back of their own hand from the back of somebody else's hand."

"That's a discouraging thought." Rachel laughed. "Just think about waking up some morning and you're wearing the backs of someone else's hands but never realizing it until it was too late."

"Too late for what?"

"I don't know, just too late."

His eyes were still on the beach. "Sounds like a science-fiction story. But I think we've got some other kind of story going on." And he pointed toward the beach. The shapes of men were visible in the trees. "We can't turn around in this channel, right?"

"We can't turn around."

Thomas Ashbrooke picked up the little waterproof case for the MP5-K submachine gun and started to unzip it. "Get below."

Chapter Twelve

*T*here were no guards inside the truck with them. And the reason seemed obvious. They were powerless to escape their bonds. Plastic restraints of the type used by antiriot personnel for mass arrests were used instead of rope, the kind of restraints that could only be cut off, not untied, fabricated of some high tensile–strength material yet very thin, the result being that one could not even attempt to tear them apart without gouging the flesh until it bled.

Several of the men had tried.

Once the officers were herded up into the trucks, two M-16-armed guards positioned themselves at the rear of the truck while two other men, weaponless, started at the front of the trailer and moved rearward, affixing identical plastic restraints to the prisoners, but in a way Colonel Young had never seen before. The farthest forward man's farthest forward ankle was left unbound, his other ankle bound to the ankle of the man seated on the bench beside him. The farthest rearward man's farthest rearward ankle—if he sat on the right side of the truck, his left ankle—was also left unbound.

The prisoners were locked together as if they were about to participate in some enormous, multilegged sack race.

Once again male and female personnel were segregated, as were officers segregated from the comparatively few noncoms, but there was no distinction made from one service branch to the other, marines (like himself) mixed together with coasties, air force, army, and navy.

The truck in which Young and the twenty-three officers with him rode at last stopped.

Nothing happened for several minutes.

"Think we're there, sir?" Young looked to the air force captain beside him, Young's left ankle lashed to the captain's right. "I'm sure tired of just sitting."

Young smiled good-naturedly. "Then why'd you join the air force in the first place?"

The captain laughed.

Young said, "I hope we're there."

As if to resolve the matter, the doors of the truck were opened, a rush of cool, fresh air sending a shiver along Young's spine.

Framed in the opening was Captain Brandon, along with him a half dozen other Presidential Strike Force personnel, except for Brandon everyone armed with an M-16. "Thought we'd give you and your men a chance to walk around a little, Colonel. Still a couple of hours to the billeting area."

"Thank you." Young nodded curtly.

"Sure thing, sir." Brandon smiled. Two more men appeared, weaponless, climbing up into the rear of the truck, walking the length of it forward, then producing pocket-sized wire cutters. They began clipping the bindings that held the men's ankles together.

Thomas Ashbrooke took one last look through the binoculars. The men waiting in the rocks and palm trees beyond the beach—they were making no attempt to hide—could have been anyone from drug smugglers to the FLNA to U.S. forces working under the orders of

Roman Makowski and his security director, Hobart Townes, to the friendlies he'd been hoping to find, men and women from the Miami Patriot cell under Gulliermo Martine.

He handed off the binoculars in disgust to the former drug smuggler who had the helm, then he started below. Rachel was in the salon, her left foot up on the arm of the sofa. She had changed out of white cotton slacks and a navy-blue T-shirt into a pink sundress of a soft floral print with a very full skirt. The dress's skirt was well above her thigh as she looked up, smiled at him, then returned to her work. She was attaching the leg strap of some kind of thigh holster. "Wait for me before you go on deck," Ashbrooke warned her. "If they're bad guys, they could start the thing anytime. We're still a little out in the channel for handguns or subguns, but you never know what they might have."

"Yes, Thomas" was all she said, taking up a stainless-steel Walther PPK in her hands, beginning to check the magazine.

Ashbrooke walked along the companionway, stopping at his unlocked cabin door, opening the door and entering. The suitcase he had under the bed had everything he needed inside. He pulled it out, slung it onto the mattress, and opened it.

Ashbrooke slipped off his windbreaker, threw it down onto the bed. He shrugged out of his shoulder holster as well.

From the suitcase, Ashbrooke picked up the Galco Stalker rig for the 870, began slinging it on where the shoulder holster had been seconds ago. He took the 870 from the case and checked the magazine. Five rounds loaded, two- and three-quarter-inch-high brass Double O Buck. The gun had been legal where he'd purchased it and had it altered but wasn't legal here. But of course almost no guns were legal in the United States these days. The 870's barrel was cut back to just in front of the magazine tube, its length now twelve and one-half inches when measured from the front of the receiver. The 870 was fitted with a Pachmayr Vindicator kit, giving it a pistol grip not dissimilar in feel from an N-Frame Smith & Wesson revolver. He inserted the sawed-off shotgun's receiver into the suede-lined Kydex holster, the gun hanging under his right arm now.

He looked to his left side, checking the spring-loaded shell carrier that contained six more rounds of shot.

That accomplished, Ashbrooke crossed his cabin to the closet, took down a lightweight khaki sport coat and pulled it on, the coat just long enough to hide the shotgun's muzzle and just loose-fitting enough to keep its bulk from profiling under the fabric.

Ashbrooke went back to the bed. He put his left foot up on the footboard and began binding the ankle holster around his calf, then checked the little SIG-Sauer P-228's condition of readiness and holstered it, tugging his pants leg back down. From the case he took two spare magazines for the larger 226 that he normally carried in the shoulder holster. He gave the top rounds in each magazine a downward push, testing magazine spring quality, then slapped each magazine's spine in turn against the palm of his left hand, giving a final seating to the cartridges.

He dropped one magazine into each side pocket of his loose-fitting slacks, then snatched the full-sized SIG from the holster and slipped it behind his left hipbone, butt forward so he could get at it with his right-hand cross draw or his left hand in a reverse draw. The magazines, although they'd stick out a bit below the grip frame, would work equally well with the smaller SIG 9mm he'd recently acquired.

Ashbrooke stopped for a second to look at himself in

the full-length mirror mounted on the closet door, to see if any of what he carried showed. Nothing did. And he took notice of his white hair. "Getting too old for this shit, Thomas," Ashbrooke told his reflection.

Then he started out of the cabin, without any rebuttal. And he guessed that was a good thing.

Wood noticed that the bleeding of his left thigh had stopped. He knew that once he got moving again, the bleeding would likely resume. But he had no intention of moving any more until dark. The woods were thick with Presidential Strike Force personnel but no police.

On a rational basis, he interpreted the absence of police or any other military personnel beyond the PSF as indicating that the PSF was desirous of keeping what they were doing strictly to themselves, which meant that if he could get to help and spread the word of what had happened he might strike a serious blow to the Presidential Strike Force and the dictator whose policy they served.

On an emotional basis, he wanted to jump out of the tree into which he had climbed and onto the back of the first PSF-er who passed below him, throttling the man to death as some measure of revenge for Red's murder.

When he closed his eyes he could still see her frail-seeming body, the blood-stained blouse, the perspiration-matted red hair—and the green eyes that would never see anything ever again.

Chapter Thirteen

*R*achel wore a lightweight white unconstructed cotton jacket over her sundress, and when she put her hands in the coat's pockets, Ashbrooke could just faintly make out the outline of her shoulder holster beneath it. "You're profiling a little," Ashbrooke whispered through his teeth.

Subtly she eased the downward tension of her hands in her pockets.

The motorized launch in which they rode with three crew members in addition to the captain, all of them either Mossad, like Rachel, or Israeli commandos, like the captain, lurched violently over a swell and bottomed out for an instant, the motor grinding, then moved on.

The men in the rocks and trees beyond the beach started drifting out of the shade and closer to the surf. They were visibly armed with submachine guns. "I've always wondered how it feels to be Israeli and looking down the wrong end of an Uzi," Ashbrooke remarked almost under his breath.

Rachel whispered back, "Just as comfortable as an American feels looking down the wrong end of a .45 automatic, I suppose."

Despite the circumstances, Ashbrooke smiled.

There were Heckler & Koch MP5-K submachine guns

in the bottom of the launch in plastic bags, and each of the four men with Ashbrooke and Rachel would be armed as heavily as circumstances permitted.

The launch was almost into the surf now and Ashbrooke kicked out of his deck shoes, preparing to give his feet, the bottoms of his trouser legs, and the little SIG-Sauer 228 a dousing. He made a mental note that, if he survived whatever lay in store, he should detail disassemble the pistol and clean it at once.

As the launch started bellying onto the sand, two of the crewmen jumped out, towing it forward over a white-crested breaker.

Ashbrooke stood and helped Rachel to her feet. She, too, was barefoot. He stepped into the water, assisting Rachel out after him. The beach was classically beautiful, palm trees swaying in the same wind that toyed with Rachel's auburn hair and billowed the soft fabric of her dress around her tanned legs. The sand was almost white and very clean. Under different circumstances the setting would have been idyllic, he thought.

As they stepped out of the surf, one of the men from the center of the growing number of men there on the beach—there were seven in sight—shouted to them, "Who are you?" The voice was Spanish-accented. The two-hundred-dollar sport shirts and five-hundred-dollar slacks the men wore were the kind seen in fashion-magazine advertisements and shop windows along strips like Rodeo Drive, the automatic weapons looking factory original, all the little details Ashbrooke perceived serving to confirm his suspicions that perhaps the *Ruth II* 's ship's complement had come ashore into the middle of a deal. Columbians perhaps.

Ashbrooke answered, "We're having a little engine trouble and wanted to get in someplace safe to take a look." That was a lie, but lying under the circumstances was immaterial.

"There is no storm coming, I think."

"Hey, it never hurts to be cautious, huh? How about you guys—company picnic?" Time was, the word *company* meant different things to different people in south Florida, but that time had largely passed.

"She's a pretty woman," the man shouted to them, holding his Uzi a little more tightly but not menacingly, not yet.

"The woman can talk for herself," Rachel called back.

Ashbrooke noticed her shifting her shoulders slightly under the weight of the holster rig.

"You're an old guy to have such a woman with you. She your squeeze?"

Ashbrooke called back to him, "Well, maybe when you're my age if you're really lucky—and you live that long—you'll have one just like her, *amigo.*"

The talker laughed. Then, abruptly his laughter died and his smile died with it. "What if maybe I kill your ass and just take her—*amigo*?"

Ashbrooke just looked at him for a moment. Then he said, "We've got a meeting here, and I assume by accident, you do too. Unless you've got about fifty more guys hidden up behind those palms—and they'd have to be really skinny guys—you start a shooting war, you're in deep shit. So back off—*amigo.*"

The talker looked around at his friends, laughing a little, kicking his feet in the sand like a bull pawing the arena before a charge. Watching the talker's face intently, Ashbrooke started moving slowly away from the launch and away from Rachel.

"I think I decided. I'll kill you, you old son of a bitch, then take the woman. That is a good idea."

Ashbrooke stopped walking. He could get to the SIG-Sauer 226 behind his left hipbone most easily of all the weapons he was carrying. He'd met men like this before. They couldn't just start shooting but had to talk themselves into the right frame of mind for their own head and to project the right image to their compatriots. "Then I think you'd better just stop talking," Ashbrooke remarked.

The muscles around the talker's mouth and the tendons in his neck moved slightly and Thomas Ashbrooke shouted, "Now!" as he dipped his right knee outward, shifting his upper body close to two feet right. His left hand cleared his coattails enough to fist the 226 in a full combat grip as he wrenched the 9mm around.

Gunfire from the launch, one of the Heckler & Koch submachine guns, coming in the same instant as a burst from the talker's Uzi whistled past Ashbrooke's left side, just missing him. Ashbrooke was already firing, rotating the SIG's muzzle right and left and back again, using the spray-and-pray technique. He caught one of the druggies in the stomach, another of the druggies pulling the man to cover.

Ashbrooke's hand moved for the sawed-off as he ran for the nearest rocks, about six feet to his left. He caught a blur of Rachel's pink dress moving behind him from the corner of his left eye, heard the report of another 9mm pistol, assumed it was hers.

Submachine gunfire tore into the sand just in front of him as he dove behind the rocks, Rachel shouting, "I'm covering you!"

Every bone in Ashbrooke's body ached. "Damn being old!" He rolled onto his back, the empty SIG into his outside jacket pocket, the 870 coming up in his right fist.

"The one with the mouth!" Rachel almost shrieked, firing out the Walther P-88 toward the talker as he ran to new cover.

Ashbrooke's 870 was already racked and he fired, a chunk of the palm tree the talker had passed tearing away. The trouble with pistol-gripped sawed-off shot-

guns was they were hard to shoot accurately much beyond spitting distance, the price one paid, Ashbrooke
reflected, for concealability. He had the pump
tromboned again and fired a second time, catching one
of the other six druggies with a partial pellet load in the
right thigh. The man went down, scrambling to cover, a
long burst of submachine gunfire tearing into the rocks
as the man ducked behind them.

Ashbrooke looked toward the launch. Everyone was
gone from it. Beyond the launch on the far side, in the
rocky area where the surf came, he spotted the Israeli
commando who was the vessel's captain and another of
the crew members, the other Mossad agent. He gave
Ashbrooke a thumbs-up.

Submachine gunfire sprayed into the rocks behind
which Ashbrooke and Rachel Roth had taken cover and
Ashbrooke hunkered down beside Rachel. She knelt,
her dress ballooned around her like the depiction in a
painting of some turn-of-the-century girl at a lawn
party. She was putting a fresh fifteen-round magazine
up the butt of the Walther P-88 while Ashbrooke
swapped magazines in the 226. "Listen," she said.
"What are we going to do? The gunfire could attract
attention."

"It could get us killed too," Ashbrooke observed.

Rachel hitched up her dress and pulled the PPK from
the thigh holster on her left leg, a pistol in each hand
now.

Ashbrooke looked at her and felt himself grin. "All
right. We're going to have to separate into two ele-
ments. You and I'll go up on this side into the palms and
Ishmael, the Mossad guy, and one of the commandos
goes up the other side. The captain and the remaining
man can cover us from where they're at. Don't tell 'em
in English. Use Hebrew instead of Yiddish because
there are enough foreign languages spoken in Miami

that one of those guys might have picked up enough Yiddish or German to make sense out of it. Got me?"

"Right."

Ashbrooke took the smaller SIG—it hadn't gotten wet—from his ankle holster. As Rachel started repeating his orders in Hebrew, Ashbrooke stuffed the smaller SIG into his waistband beside the full-sized 226.

"Ishmael's ready whenever you say."

Ashbrooke grunted acknowledgement as he reached under his left armpit to the shell carrier, popping three twelve-gauge rounds out. He fed two of them into the 870's magazine tube, racked the pump, set the crossbolt safety by the trigger guard, and put the last round into the tube, giving him one round chambered and five more ready to go.

"Tell the captain as heavy a volume of fire as he can sustain. We have to get really close to do this. Then tell Ishmael that what we want is to get close in, within easy pistol range. So he and his man use their submachine guns and draw off fire. You and I'll come in from behind and finish the job as soon as Ishmael's got their attention. We just go up and murder them before they murder us. After you tell him that, slip into Yiddish and tell the captain to radio the *Ruth II* for more men and more guns."

"He doesn't have a radio, and we don't have that—"

"I know, but the bad guys don't. On the off chance one of them can handle enough Yiddish, the last thing they'll figure is we're going to attack in the next two minutes. Just do it."

Rachel nodded, pushed her hair back from her face, and started the flow of Hebrew again. Tom Ashbrooke peered around the rocks just as a burst of submachine gunfire tore into the sand and he pulled his face back, the sand just missing his eyes.

He heard her speaking in Yiddish, enough of which he understood from his youth.

She turned to him. "We are ready?"

"We are ready," Ashbrooke nodded. "On my signal."

Thomas Ashbrooke pulled his feet under him and got into a crouch, brushing sand off his hands against the thighs of his trouser legs. He shifted the 870 a little, working the crossbolt safety off and back on but leaving his finger out of the trigger guard. It would be close-range killing, if he got that far. Ashbrooke put the 870 into its holster under his right armpit, then drew both 9mm pistols from his waistband.

"Now!" And Ashbrooke ran, breaking left along a line of low rocks, a gun firing from each hand, Rachel beside and just a little behind him, heavy automatic-weapons covering fire from the rocks by the surf, chunks ripped out of the trunks of the palm trees where the druggies were positioned.

One of the druggies rolled out from cover, firing a short burst from his submachine gun, Ashbrooke leveling both pistols toward the man and firing simultaneously, putting him down as a spray of sand blew up toward Ashbrooke's face. He heard a scream from behind him, looked back, saw Rachel, the left sleeve of her white jacket reddening with blood. She stumbled, didn't fall, ran on. Ashbrooke slowed, momentarily taking sparse cover between two palms, drawing fire as Rachel cleared past him and was behind the higher rocks. Both of Ashbrooke's pistols were empty and he had one more magazine to load in, the 226. Then he ran for the higher rocks flanking the druggies' position where Rachel was already hidden, giving him cover fire.

Ashbrooke dropped to the sand about a yard from her. He looked past Rachel. There was a clear line of solid cover, the rocks formed up like the spinal column of some sort of huge beast reaching back toward the interior.

She was changing magazines for the P-88. "This is my last and the PPK is empty." Ashbrooke nodded, edging closer to her, turning her around so he could get a look at the arm held limply at her side. "I've been shot before. This isn't bad," she announced matter-of-factly.

"Great. Let me take a quick look at it anyway." He reached into his shirt pocket for the B&D Grande pen-shaped knife, folded out the blade, and slit the jacket sleeve neatly up the seam. "You were right, it isn't bad." She had a deep flesh wound that was bleeding a good bit but nothing more, from what he could see. He wiped the blade clean of her blood by stabbing it into the sand before he closed and pocketed it. "You up to this?"

"Of course."

"No more shooting unless you have to, until we get near enough to do some good."

"Agreed."

Ashbrooke shifted the 226 to his left hand and pulled the 870 from the Galco rig, pushing the crossbolt safety off and keeping his finger out of the trigger guard. "Come on. Ishmael might already be in position."

Ashbrooke, keeping to as much of a crouch as his back could stand, started forward, Rachel beside him. The P-88 was being stuffed into her jacket pocket as he looked at her, her right hand catching up her dress, reaching to her right thigh. She came back with a knife, one of the cheap, ultraflat throwing knives. Ashbrooke had used them—despite the throwaway price, they threw well and took an acceptable edge. Rachel clamped the knife into her even white teeth, the Walther P-88 back in her right hand again.

Ashbrooke stopped, judging they were about even with the druggies' position. There was no sign of Ishmael. "You got some signal or something so he'll know we're here?"

"Ishmael? No. He'll open fire when he is in position."

As Ashbrooke started to say something, a heavy volume of automatic-weapons fire started from the far side of the druggies' position. There was a growing volume of answering fire from within the stand of palms.

More automatic-weapons fire came from the rocks near the surf where the captain and the other Israeli commando were positioned.

"Now or never," Ashbrooke told Rachel, and he worked the 870's safety on as he started up, clambering as quickly as he could over the rocks and dropping down into the sand, losing his footing, falling to his knees. He stood, Rachel coming over. Ashbrooke started to run toward the palms, keeping to as much cover in the less dense portion of the stand as he could, the answering fire from within the stand louder.

He could feel Rachel beside him.

A man popped up from behind a half-rotted trunk bisecting a semicircular aggregate of rocks. Ashbrooke shot the man in the face with the 226.

Rachel shouted, "They are on to us!"

But Ashbrooke was already running forward, the SIG-Sauer pistol safed and stuffed into his belt, his first finger into the trigger guard of the 870 and the safety off. With the sawed-off pump at hip level, he fired into the center of mass of one of the druggies, bowling the man over.

Ashbrooke tromboned the pump.

A burst of submachine gunfire hammered into a palm trunk near him and Ashbrooke averted his eyes as he pulled the trigger again, hit the sand and rolled, gunfire churning the sand beside him. He pumped the 870, shucking the empty hull and chambering a fresh round.

It was the talker. "Fuck you, man!"

As Ashbrooke stabbed the muzzle of the sawed-off toward the talker—he knew it was too late—there was a double tap, then another from behind him. The talker staggered back, at least two rounds in his chest, the Uzi in his hands starting to spray. Ashbrooke pulled the 870's trigger, the full load of Double O Buck catching the talker in the face and rocking him back, the submachine gun firing out toward the sky.

Ashbrooke was up, pumping the 870's action again, keeping count of his shots as he ran forward. Three left, plus the three in the shoulder rig. He grabbed at these, clicking them out one at a time, feeding two of them into the 870's tubular magazine one at a time, the third one between the first and second fingers of his left hand as he might hold a fat, stubby cigar.

One of the druggies dashed from cover, a pistol in each hand, an Uzi dangling from its sling across his chest. Ashbrooke fired the shotgun, missed, cursed, pumped, fired, and caught the man across the small of the back.

The man went down, rolled, stabbed both pistols toward Ashbrooke as Ashbrooke stroked the pump. Four pistol shots rang out fast, blood spurting from the druggie's left temple and cheek.

Tom Ashbrooke fed the last round into the 870, giving him a total of five left.

"I'm empty," he heard Rachel sing out.

"Grab an Uzi."

"I am."

There was no movement. For an instant Ashbrooke thought all the druggies were dead.

"Thomas!"

Ashbrooke wheeled left, a man running for him, an Uzi in his right hand, his left arm and the left side of his chest oozing blood. As Ashbrooke fired, something flashed past him. The pellets from Ashbrooke's sawed-

off and Rachel's throwing knife hit the druggie simultaneously, it seemed, the man's body rocking back against
a palm trunk as Ashbrooke, the pump tromboned,
started to fire again.

But there was no reason. The knife had the man in
the chest, the shotgun had caught him in the abdomen,
and his eyes were wide-open dead eyes.

"No time for that Uzi," Rachel observed.

Thomas Ashbrooke breathed. "You bet." The SIG
was back in his left hand, the 870 still in his right as he
moved cautiously forward. "Ishmael?"

"Over here, Mr. Ashbrooke!"

"I think we nailed them all."

"I counted ten men—that was three who didn't come
onto the beach!"

Ashbrooke nodded to himself. If he'd had a free
hand, he could have taken his pulse instead of just feeling it thrumming on the side of his neck.

This was a younger man's game to begin with, but it
kept you young doing it—so long as you didn't die trying.

Chapter Fourteen

*T*hey had been a long time out of the trucks and it was getting on toward dusk. His hands were numb from the wrist down, and if they looked like the hands of the young air force captain who stood near him—the man's name was Johnson—they were purple from lack of circulation.

Young tried flexing his fingers.

"What are they doing, Colonel?"

"What?" Young looked at Captain Johnson, then followed Johnson's eyes toward the small van that had just pulled up. Weapons were being handed out of the van to the PSF personnel bunching around it.

Quickly Young looked around them. At least two dozen PSFs had them surrounded, M-16s held at sloppy port arms, but ready.

Young looked back toward the truck.

The guns were as heterogeneous an assortment as he had ever seen—revolvers, lever-action rifles, bolt actions with scopes, a few shotguns, some obvious .22s, both target pistols and rifles, a number of .45 automatics like those that, until recently, had been the service standard for all branches, with the exception of specialized units such as air police and the like.

"Colonel?"

"I don't know, Johnson," Young said under his breath.

The PSF personnel near the van were inspecting the weapons, loading them, shouldering them or otherwise hefting them as if preparing to fire.

Young shouted across the clearing toward Captain Brandon, the PSF commander. "Captain? When are we getting aboard the trucks again so we can move out?"

Captain Brandon turned away from the senior non-com he was talking to. He looked but said nothing, then turned away and walked toward the van. Young's eyes never left Brandon. Brandon looked inside the van and then reached inside. When he turned around there was a bolt-action rifle in his hands. He cycled the bolt, shouldered the rifle, then proceeded to load the rifle.

As he finished he looked toward Young, at the top of his lungs ordering, "Fall your men in, Colonel. Now."

Young licked his lips. Johnson hissed under his breath, "I don't like this, not a damn—"

"Neither do I, Captain." And Young raised his voice, calling to Captain Brandon, "What are you planning?"

"Funny thing you should ask, Colonel. Fall your men in or die where you stand." Brandon shouldered the rifle.

Young shivered.

He looked around. The men with the M-16s had raised their rifles to their shoulders.

Young looked at Brandon. "You can't be—"

"Yes, as a matter of fact, Colonel, I sure as hell can. And the best part is that with all of these oddball calibers—these are guns we've confiscated under the Executive Order—with all these different calibers, it's gonna look just like we want it to."

"I don't—" Young started.

"Like the Patriots, Colonel, like the Patriots killed all of you."

"Katyn Forest," Young whispered under his breath, then shouted to the one hundred ninety-two men and women in the clearing, "Run for it! Run! They're going to shoo—"

The old stories were wrong, Young thought as he fell and his lids became so heavy that he couldn't raise them and the blackness enveloped him. You could hear the shot that killed you.

Chapter Fifteen

Wood was cold, terribly cold. He told himself that the source of his discomfort was probably a combination of the natural coolness of the fall night and the loss of blood from his wound. He did not want to consider that the chills he felt were symptomatic of an infection. The wound had opened up again—not much, he thought, though—before he'd gone a hundred yards. Probably climbing out of the tree hadn't helped either.

The trees were thinning out and he thought he might be nearing a road. But then where?

He knew almost precisely (as precisely as someone could without a compass or wristwatch or other device) in which direction he had traveled, but since he had no idea of what might be in his immediate vicinity, a sense of direction was useless. When he reached the road, if it was a road, he'd flip the same mental coin he'd flipped when he'd come down out of the tree and determined in which direction to move.

The Presidential Strike Force troopers had moved out a little after dark and Wood had waited for quite a long time after that, quietly waited in his tree, to make certain they had really gone and it wasn't just some kind of trick to lure him out.

But at last he convinced himself they had really given

up, perhaps assuming that he and Red had split up before they'd found her, shot her down.

Just thinking of that now brought the tightness back into his throat. She was dead and he was alive.

Damn them, he thought, moving steadily among the trees.

It was, in fact, a road.

He didn't leave the treeline, didn't even contemplate crossing it, could see no light in either direction. But it was a two-lane blacktop and flat and had to lead between two points.

Wood flipped his mental coin, then started north.

Chapter Sixteen

*T*he typical woman's hand-eye coordination was superior to that of the typical man. Considering that Linda Effingham had virtually no experience at all with firearms, she had not done badly at all.

Kearney glanced over toward her now. She was cuddled up into the front passenger bucket of the Suburban, belted in against a sudden stop, beneath his heavy winter coat. He saw the smile on her lips and flicked off the overhead map light nearest him.

A glance down at the Suburban's speedometer confirmed that he was well within the fifty-five-mile-per-hour speed limit for the road they were traveling. And as he glanced into the rearview, then lit a Pall Mall in the blue-yellow flame of the lighter—it was a solid brass full-sized Zippo, scratched and corroded but perfectly and reliably functional—he pondered why, in a country teetering on the edge of full-scale revolution, with a terrorist problem despite the announced FLNA cease-fire earlier in the day, would any police officer in his right mind waste time and energy waiting for some hapless speeder.

Geoffrey Kearney knew the answer. Police officers, like soldiers and—he smiled at the thought—like British agents, followed orders. At least usually.

He'd found the most remote spot he could safely get

into with the Suburban, then gone farther into the woods on foot for nearly a mile, found a clearing, and set up teaching Linda some of the fundamentals of pistol marksmanship. He'd given her the S & W 5904 to use, identical to the 5906 with which he'd replaced it in every way but metallurgical.

At twenty-one feet she could keep everything into something six-by-six inches if she took her time. And that wasn't bad for a first time out. Some of the shots, when viewed as subsets of the whole, had produced two- and even three-round groups under two inches.

Definite promise.

As he inhaled again on his cigarette, Geoffrey Kearney told himself that he was a fool. If he loved Linda that much—and he did—there had to be someplace safer for her than at his side. Because his job had to be done.

"Nuts," he hissed as he exhaled.

"What?"

"Go back to sleep, darling."

"I was just resting my eyes."

"Right." Kearney laughed.

"Are we there yet?"

Kearney laughed aloud. Women were sometimes so beautifully like children. If they were there, as she'd put it, why would they still be driving? "No. Go back to sleep."

"Why? Are you trying to think something through?"

"More or less."

"About what?"

"What I'm going to do with you while I find Dimitri Borsoi so I can kill the bloody bastard."

"I—"

"No, whatever it is you're about to suggest. We'll go side by side, like the old song says, but once I'm near

Borsoi you're going to ground, I'm afraid. I'd never be able to get a man like him, having to worry about you."

There was a little catch in her throat as she spoke after a moment's pause. "Are you sorry I'm with you, Geoff?"

"No."

Chapter Seventeen

*R*achel sat beside him, the flesh wound to her left arm cleaned, medicated, bandaged, and in a sling. He draped the heavy sweater over her shoulders that he had gone below decks to retrieve when she'd said she was cold. Her knees were almost up to her chin and her dress pulled down so it covered her bare feet.

The *Ruth II* swayed on its moorings, an anchor out astern and off the bow.

"If any of us die here, you must promise me that you will have the body burned so it can never be identified."

Ashbrooke just looked at her for a moment in the light of the lamp swinging from the jib near them. "All right, Rachel. If I'm alive to do it."

She nodded, saying nothing, apparently satisfied.

Laboriously, after first having taken care of what emergency treatment was required for Rachel's arm and the captain's left leg—he'd picked up two bullets in his thigh—they had hauled the bodies of the dead druggies, three at a time, out to the *Ruth II*. Then their reformed-druggie pilot had gotten them back out of the channel and into open water.

Weighted down with whatever was available, the dead men were heaved overboard. Rachel, a trained nurse, after having gotten help seeing to her own arm so she would be functional, had dug the bullets out of the captain's leg and sedated him. There was some muscle damage and there would be considerable discomfort, but barring infection or other unforeseen complications he would recover.

Then they'd backed the *Ruth II* into the channel after having determined that the gunfire from the battle with the drug smugglers hadn't attracted police or military attention.

And now they waited, waited for the representatives of the Miami-based Patriot cell to arrive.

The Uzis and other weapons taken from the dead druggies would be given over to the Miami Patriots as a pot-sweetener for their help in smuggling in the weapons already aboard the *Ruth II,* only a portion of which was destined for them.

Automatic weapons were of vital importance to the Patriots since the arrival on the American scene of Roman Makowski's Presidential Strike Force. The PSF had all the equipment it needed, but the Patriots had only the automatic weapons recovered in the aftermath of battle from the Front for the Liberation of North America. Period.

Contrary to media propaganda and the public opinion it generated in some quarters, the Patriots were not heavily armed and most of the firearms the Patriots did have were conventional semiautomatics at best, in the main a disorganized hodgepodge of odd-caliber bolt actions and lever actions, sporting arms often ill-suited to combat. Among these, with the exception of military-similar arms such as Uzi carbines, AR-15 Sporters and the like, extra parts, even spare magazines and, of growing concern, ammunition were impossible to replace. The supply of ammunition in popular but strictly civilian calibers, such as .30–30, .30–06, even .22 Long Rifle, was drying up since its sale was prohibited and manufacture was, therefore, all but suspended.

The principal source of ammunition supply for the Patriots was, again, what could be stolen from the FLNA, the FLNA having previously either smuggled needed items into the country or stolen material from government arsenals or cross-country shipments.

With the entry of a heavily armed force—the Presidential Strike Force—with a limitless supply network backing it up, the already tenuous situation for the Patriots became worse. Hence this, the first of what Thomas Ashbrooke intended to be numerous arms shipments, this one quite small and acquired at considerable expense. Size would have to increase and a means for financing the arms shipments be developed.

Since this first shipment was so small, only items that would prove of immediate utility to the Metro Patriot cell were incorporated—submachine guns and assault rifles, spare-parts kits, spare magazines, and as much ammunition as the *Ruth II* could carry without slowing her down to dangerously slow speed.

A drop in the bucket, as the old expression went.

"What are you thinking about, Thomas?"

"How futile all of this is compared to the task that lies ahead."

"Your wife—Diane?—is a very fortunate woman. Men like you come along very rarely."

Ashbrooke laughed. "She might count herself more fortunate if I were back home with her in Switzerland right now."

Rachel, no humor in her voice, said, "I seriously doubt that, Thomas. From what you've told me of her, I'd say she is, however worried she might be, very proud of you. To do this for a son-in-law—"

"No," Ashbrooke told her, lighting a cigarette. "No, see, I mean I'm helping—or trying to help—David's Patriot group in Metro, yeah, but it's not just because it's David. Now, I admit, he's probably what got me involved in the whole thing, granted, but that's not why I'm sticking with it. This is a good country, Rachel, a place like no other country. And if it goes down the drain, falls, well—there'll never be another one like it."

Rachel rubbed at her arm, locked her good hand around her legs again. "Why do you live in Switzerland?"

Ashbrooke laughed. "That's a very long story. I guess, to boil it down, I'd have to say maybe I saw this coming and told myself I could escape it, live out my days with my wife in peace. Terrorism was bound to plague the United States, and there was no country in the world less able to cope with it. But the reasons the U.S. was so unable to handle it were the very reasons that the country was as great as it was. I guess," Ashbrooke told her, not looking at her, but watching the blackness of the water surrounding them, "that I lied to myself that I could just run away from the problems I knew were coming. I couldn't though."

Rachel started to speak, but the Mossad man, Ishmael, shouted from the prow, "I think they are coming, the contacts!"

Ashbrooke stood, grabbing up one of the MP5-K submachine guns. People were coming out of the stand of palms where earlier that evening the gun battle had taken place, about a dozen people, the light so poor that at the distance his eyes couldn't even distinguish men from women.

But a red starburst flare was fired into the sky.

Ashbrooke heard the pilot's voice calling out softly where he sat beside the radio. "It's them, Mr. Ashbrooke. They gave that dumbass code phrase."

Ashbrooke looked toward the man, barely able to make out his features because he sat in shadow out of the light of the lantern. If he hadn't already held the pilot in contempt, he would have now. The code phrase was a line from the Pledge of Allegiance: ". . . one nation, under God, indivisible . . ."

Chapter Eighteen

*T*here was a boy standing on the back porch.

"Hey, kid," Wood hissed.

The boy might not have heard him.

"Son."

The boy's hands had been in his jacket pockets for the several minutes Wood had observed him. He wore only a windbreaker, which didn't look warm enough to fend off the night's chill. Now the boy's hands were out of his pockets, slightly away from his sides, and as he looked toward the fence there was an attitude to his body like that of a coiled spring ready to pop—or a frightened boy ready to run. From the far side of the fence, Wood called to him again. "Son, I need some help. Could you help me, please?"

The boy didn't move, but after a second or two he spoke. "My mom and dad are inside."

A warning or an offer of assistance? A warning, Wood decided. "Look, son. I'm in trouble. And I'm hurt. If your mom and dad are—" How should he put it to a kid? Was Red right when she said their only chance was the Patriots? "Answer me straight, son. I'm an army officer and I'm in big trouble. Do your mom and dad know anybody who's in the Patriots?"

The boy just stood there for a moment, then started toward the back-porch door.

Wood called after him. "Hey, son. I'm looking for the Patriots, so I can tell them something important. I'm shot and I'm bleeding and—"

The boy disappeared into the house and slammed the back door after him.

Wood sagged heavily against the fence. It was impossible for him to sit, because his leg would not bend, and if he could sit down he was afraid he would not be able to get up again. Wood just stood there.

His ideals, he realized, were ebbing from him like his blood. That he should have asked a young boy to help lead him to an armed band that took the law into its own hands in defiance of regularly constituted authority at once shocked and amazed him.

He'd walked along the hard-packed dirt track that passed for an urban alleyway between the two rows of houses at the outskirts of the small town, looked for some hopeful sign or even a normal lighted window. There were lights everywhere, to be sure, masked behind dark, heavy drapes like the blackout curtains he'd seen in movies about World War Two. But no warm windows into an island of normalcy, only pencil-thin bars of light from homes where people were afraid and waited in fear for the unthinkable to search them out and destroy them.

Then he'd seen the boy. The boy was just standing there, watching the night. In dark clothes, the boy could easily have been missed. But Wood had seen him, approached the fence, waited there, observing him.

Was there any hope left?

Wood started away from the fence, dragging his left leg now because it was even stiffer.

Into the rutted dirt alleyway again, Wood quickened his pace. The boy's parents might have called the police.

"Hey!"

Wood froze.

The voice that called from behind him was not the voice of a boy.

"Yeah, I'm talkin' to you. What's wrong with your leg?"

Wood turned around slowly.

"You look like you're in trouble, fella," the man—about forty or so, Wood thought—said after a moment.

"Sir, I—"

Wood fell over, slamming into the dirt as he closed his eyes.

Chapter Nineteen

David Holden opened his eyes and looked at Rosie. "What is—"

"Mitch Diamond on the radio." Her voice was a soft alto whisper, the touch of her fingertips cool against his bare shoulder.

"Ohh." Holden nodded, still half asleep. He couldn't see Rosie and assumed Rosie couldn't see him, but he nodded in the near-total darkness anyway. "All right. I'll get up." Holden sat up, nodding uselessly again as Rosie Shepherd handed him his pants.

David Holden zipped the front of his black M-65 field jacket against the predawn cold. He wore no shirt, no underpants, no socks, just his boots—unlaced—and his BDU pants and the jacket. Rosie, beside him, was attired similarly, except for the addition of a black T-shirt. The harness for Holden's shoulder holster was slung to his right shoulder only, and as they entered the communications tent, Rosie going through the flap opening ahead of him, he took the rig with the smaller of the two Beretta pistols, two spare magazines, and the Crain Defender knife and set it on the table.

Patsy Alfredi was standing inside the semicircle of camp tables for the radios. She picked up one of several clipboards and started to hand it to Holden.

"Read it, Patsy," Holden told her.

She nodded. Then, "I'm not waiting for an okay on this. I have a man you have to see right away. Get prepared for a long day. I'll be there around dawn." She looked up from the clipboard. "It's from Mitch. He didn't say anything else."

David Holden looked at the Rolex on his left wrist: *. . . a long day.* Holden looked at Rosie. "Start getting everybody up. I want the unit commanders in the command tent in thirty minutes." He looked at Patsy. "Keep me posted if you hear anything more from Mitch."

"Right." She nodded.

. . . A long day. That was a code phrase with the Patriot movement indicating to prepare for a major operation or engagement.

David Holden drank coffee. He was colder now than he had been, his hair wet from the shower. The coffee was hot.

The camp showers were the type where the water was warmed by the heat of the sunlight. At this time of the morning, before dawn, there was no sun to warm the water and the water was icy cold. A propane-based water-heating system was under construction for the camp, but whether it would be completed in time to be used before it became necessary, for security reasons, to move on again was another question.

Women, statistically, seemed better able to withstand greater temperature extremes than men but seemed more sensitive to sudden temperature shifts. Because of this latter characteristic, Holden had felt terribly sorry for Rosie, her skin goose-bumped as she'd showered with him, her hair wetter than his now as they waited for the rest of the unit leaders to assemble, her arms hugged across her breasts, and her knees clamped together tightly. There was a towel wrapped around her head, but he doubted that helped and it made her look extremely silly. Black BDUs, combat boots, some of her weapons belted on, and a pink floral-print towel bound over her hair like some sort of turban.

More of the section leaders were filtering in, about two minutes remaining before the meeting would start. Holden still thought of the men and women who were his field commanders as unit or section leaders, resisting the idea of taking on a military title for himself or giving military-rank designations to any of the personnel under his command within the cell.

At least one of the Patriot cells had its own general, although the most common designation was *colonel,* which seemed to be almost as magic-sounding a title of rank for an overall commander as *captain* for a leader in the field. For some reason, the rank of general imparted the idea of age and gray hair and separation from the field, safe behind the lines. Reflecting on his own naval career, he'd always thought that way about admirals.

Luther Steel and Bill Runningdeer entered the tent, Luther taking a cup of coffee, Runningdeer smiling— still half asleep–looking—as he took a cup as well.

Patsy Alfredi came into the tent, nodded, saying, "Tommy's watching the telephone." She sometimes referred to the radio set as that, frequently eliciting a smile or a laugh. "And I just got word from Mitch. He's on the way up, should be here inside of ten minutes."

"Good," Holden nodded. His watch indicated that it was nearly time for the meeting to commence and Patsy was the last of the necessary personnel. "All right. I don't have any idea what Mitch has cooking, who he's bringing up here. I'm not ordering a full alert, but I want the personnel about to get involved with training of the recruits we got in from the internment camp down at the fairgrounds to step down from that duty, move the schedule back a day. Give the recruits a day off. Let 'em sleep late. I was planning on that anyway. The new people want to get started and God knows we need the manpower, but they need the rest more. If we're into something, the recruits'll just get in the way for the most part, and we don't have enough arms for them anyway. If nothing serious is up, it's no big loss. Patsy?"

Patsy Alfredi looked up from her coffee.

"I know you've been on duty all night. So leave Tommy on the phones, then assign a stand-by unit ready to supplement the regular perimeter-guard detail, and then get some sleep."

"Right, David."

"David?"

Holden looked at Rosie, inclined his head toward her.

She had the towel off her head, finished rubbing her hair with it, set it down. "I think we need to bring up something David and I were talking about." And she looked at Holden. Holden inclined his head toward her again. "That's the weapons problem. David's father-in-law, Tom Ashbrooke—and that name goes no farther than this tent—he's bringing in the first load of overseas arms. And we need them. The reason we shouldn't mention his name outside of this tent is that we haven't had any facility to check out some of the new people we've been getting in. It's only a matter of time before we catch a fink." The dozen men and women crowded into the tent nodded or grumbled in the affirmative. "These weapons Tom's bringing in will be high-tech, state-of-the-art stuff. Only our most effective combat personnel will be equipped with them. And we'll use them for the obvious raid the government's expecting us to pull on that underground facility Luther turned us on to."

Luther Steel cleared his throat.

Rosie nodded toward him.

"All I want to say is that I think the underground facility is safe. Nothing was written down about it, so there's no way Makowski or that stooge of his, Townes, should know anything about it. It was a Delta flight base. There's got to be stuff buried in somebody's records about it, but if we can penetrate it soon enough, we should be able to clean it of the weapons and electronics before anybody realizes we're there."

"Soon enough is the problem, Luther," Holden told the commanders assembled in the tent. "If the base is clear, sensational. If it isn't and we don't go in force, we'll get creamed. We have to wait for the new weapons."

"I'd love to take over that facility," Rosie said almost to herself. "But like David's implying, if we got attacked while we were inside it, we wouldn't have a chance. That trashes the idea. Until we do get the weapons being smuggled in to us and have the muscle we need to hit that Delta flight installation, we're going to have to improvise. And David and I were talking about that. There's a Presidential Strike Force base set up in Metro in the old Sheik Theater."

"That was a pretty place," Patsy Alfredi said almost wistfully.

Rosie nodded. "It was. They made it look like a Middle Eastern sultan's palace. And now the PSF's using it. The ground floor is the actual base headquarters—it's their regional interrogation center. The basement area where the smoking lounge and the lower-level washrooms were is a small detention center for important prisoners under interrogation. The balconies have been converted to storage of contraband. Contraband translates into guns and ammunition and anything else the PSF takes a fancy to when they bust into somebody's house on a weapons raid, stuff like silverware, jewelry, watches, expensive stuff. Anyway, we can access the Sheik Theater by the tunnel system under the abandoned central section of Metro."

David Holden remembered the tunnels. His first real engagement as a member of the Patriots had been there. They'd hit the tunnel complex—an FLNA stronghold—several times. And the cost of doing business there had always been high.

Rosie went on. "We should be able to get all the small arms and ammo we can carry and escape into the tunnels. It'll be irregular stuff but enough to arm at least a hundred more of us on an interim basis." She lit a cigarette, saying through a cloud of smoke, "I know what some of you are thinking. It's okay for us to liberate stuff from the FLNA, and now with the Presidential Strike Force thrown against us, we'll go into the same situation with them. But this'd be taking stuff that was stolen from people just like ourselves. I figure it this way. If we take the arms and use them to fight against the FLNA and the PSF, it's better than letting them be sold off overseas to line Townes's pockets—which is what we hear has been happening—or melted down or some shit like that."

"Agreed," Holden said.

"How do we escape after we pull the raid?" Bill Runningdeer asked.

David Holden took one of Rosie's cigarettes, lit it with her lighter, and told the ex-FBI agent and the others, "We know the tunnels very well by now. So does the FLNA. We can slip in and slip out and, the PSF follows us into the tunnels, we have the decided advantage. Mitch Diamond's arranging for truck transport that will take care of us and the arms and ammunition. Anything else of obvious value gets left behind. We take the prisoners who are being held there—shouldn't be more than a dozen people and we'll have medical attention available for any who need it on an immediate basis—and we blow the theater. I hate to destroy a landmark, but I hate even worse leaving the PSF all the other valuables there and the arms we can't carry out. Any problems with that?"

"If this war ever ends," Patsy Alfredi said thoughtfully, staring into her coffee cup, "I think we're better off knowing we tried to throw a monkey wrench into the PSF than having a beautiful old building."

The tent flap opened and Mitch Diamond walked in. "David."

"Mitch. Where's your man?"

"In the back of my truck. He needs medical attention. He's stabilized, but he needs a change of bandages and like that. Better follow me out."

Luther Steel held the tent flap open for Patsy and some of the others, Holden and Rosie Shepherd the last to exit the tent.

Mists rolled off the compound grounds and the sky was grayish-violet and there was enough light to see now. Once again Holden shivered in the cold, the tent having become warm in comparison to the outside.

Rosie huddled beside Holden as Mitch Diamond's oversized hands wrenched open the tailgate and the swing-down window for the Chevy pickup's pop-top.

On the bed lay a man wrapped in blankets. Mitch shone a light from a pocket flash onto him. "Relax, Lieutenant. You're among friends at last."

The eyes opened slowly as Rosie left Holden's side and climbed up into the truck bed.

Mitch Diamond, his voice low, a little choked-sounding, said, "His name's Barnabas Wood, and he's a lieutenant in the army. He and a female air force officer escaped from a train where a whole mess of officers from all branches—some senior noncoms too—were being kept. Boxcars, like cattle. Armed PSF watchin' 'em.

No charges, no nothin'. A kid spotted him. His dad—
you know Bill Heppelwhite, I think, some of ya—anyway, Bill went after him, and the lieutenant here just
collapsed from loss of blood. The woman officer was
killed sometime yesterday, sounds like around noon.

"The lieutenant here and the woman who got killed,"
Mitch went on, "made a break for it when the train
stopped. In Metro somewhere. The prisoners were off-
loaded and the hoses were brought to clean out the cars.
The lieutenant's mission was to go for help. His colonel
—a marine named Young—figured there had to be more
trains like it, just toolin' around, loaded with officers
loyal to the Constitution and on Makowski's shitlist.
Looks to me like Hobart Townes is plannin'—what do
they call it, David?"

David Holden took his eyes from the ghostly pale
young army officer and looked at Mitch Diamond,
snapping his cigarette away as he said, "A purge."

Chapter Twenty

When he opened his eyes he was certain that, as he'd initially suspected, he was dead. Because there was an angel standing over him. But he wondered why she was dressed in black.

As Barnabas Wood looked at her more closely, he noticed that she wore some sort of uniform, all black, and a white equipment harness—no, it was a shoulder holster—over the black shirt. He'd read stories of how the Vikings and other warlike cultures had designated a special heaven to be set aside for warriors.

Was she an angel? Or was she another warrior?

He felt flattered but also was worried that there was some sort of mistake. To be in a warrior's heaven was a great honor (he supposed), but he was certain that he didn't deserve it. After all, try as he had, he had not succeeded in his mission, gotten the information out— What had the information been again?

He remembered! About Colonel Young and the others aboard that awful train and what the PSF was . . .

The blackness came again. The PSF. They were wearing field-gray uniforms, lightning bolts on their collar tabs, death's-head hat brass. That officer, the captain. The captain had a Luger in his hand and a swastika armband on his sleeve. Wood looked at his own sleeve. There was a Star of David on his sleeve and he was suddenly surrounded by a sea of people, all with their heads shaved and Stars-of-David armbands and they were being herded off a train.

Dogs—big, drooling shepherds and glistening black Dobermans with rippling musculature—snapped at them.

"Hey, this can't happen here," he shouted.

The dogs came at him and the captain fired his Luger and the darkness came.

Rose Shepherd looked away from the boy. He had lapsed into unconsciousness after having looked up at her briefly. He didn't look peaceful in his dreams, his eyelids fluttering, his face turning right and left. She touched his face with her hands, whispered to him, "It'll be all right. Just rest."

It was his fever, she realized, and Mildred Shapiro, who served as the camp physician, had given him something to bring it down. Hopefully it would work.

"Mildred?"

"Rosie?"

"Think he's gonna be okay?" Mildred was examining what looked like part of somebody's jaw. "What are you doing?"

"I want to keep an eye on the lieutenant, just in case what I gave him doesn't do the trick. Remember something, I'm a dentist. Not an MD. But the stuff's supposed to work. Meanwhile I'm still a dentist and with Mitch Diamond in today I can put that crown in for him."

"How can you stand to do that?" Rose Shepherd shivered.

"I'm helping people be healthy. How could you stand being a cop before all this?"

Rose just looked across at her. One of the few solid structures remaining in the encampment, the medical building was also the largest. When Rose Shepherd had occasion to go there, she tended to pace a lot. She'd walked all the way to the other side of the room, stopped, and answered. "I figured I was doin' something good, bein' a cop, I mean."

"That's the same way I feel about being a dentist. You realize how much pain and discomfort I can save somebody over the course of her life just by getting her to floss her teeth every day? Something as simple as that. We have kids being born here. Fine. The revolution, or whatever we're in, lasts five years or ten years or twenty. What the hell will these kids do when they're adults and they have a mouth that looks like nature hit 'em with a baseball bat? Well, they won't be able to blame me. A person can't fight with bad teeth, not well at least."

Rose Shepherd laughed. "You're tough, Mildred."

Mildred looked back to her work, Mitch's crown. "I'm not tough, I'm just trying to keep my sanity."

Rose lit a cigarette, started for the blanket hung over the doorframe that led to the small hallway beyond.

Mildred Shapiro called after her. "Smoking stains your teeth, stains your lungs, cuts down on your breathing capacity, and can kill you."

Rose Shepherd left the room.

There were other things that could kill her, too, and a lot faster than smoking would. Based on the story the unconscious young lieutenant had related to Mitch Diamond before passing out from his wound, a full-scale operation was being mounted to verify what had happened and to free the remaining personnel aboard the train, if the train could be found.

If.

And doing that meant going head-to-head with the PSF.

* * *

Luther Steel's fingers closed over the SIG-Sauer P-226's magazine as he started feeding cartridges under the lips. Bill Runningdeer, across the small table from him under the cold morning sunshine was using a loading tool to fill his Uzi submachine gun's twenty-five-round magazines. Bill Runningdeer was a devotee of the Uzi, had carried it on numerous occasions before, along with Steel, LeFleur, Blumenthal, and the still-recovering Clark Pietrowski until circumstances had forced them to leave the Federal Bureau of Investigation. According to Runningdeer—and when it concerned the Uzi, Runningdeer's word was tantamount to speaking with a chief factory engineer—the twenty-five-round magazines were the very best to use.

"You, now," Runningdeer began, as if having considered something inwardly for some time and just now having arrived at a significant conclusion, "if my people had had these available to them instead of bows and arrows, just think what the differences would be. Your ancestors never would have been captured in Africa and sold into slavery in America, because the white man never would have taken the continent. And we wouldn't be sitting here right now in the middle of a war."

Steel looked up from the SIG magazine he was loading and felt himself start to smile. "Yes, but we wouldn't be friends, would we? Because we never would have met."

Runningdeer just laughed and Steel returned to loading magazines.

Rose Shepherd crossed the compound, looking for David first in the command tent, then in the radio tent, finally deciding to try the small tent they shared together.

As she opened the flap she found him there on his knees, a ground cloth spread over a blanket before him, the Desert Eagle .44 Magnum autoloader he carried— one of two that he had, this one bequeathed him by Rufus Burroughs, the man who had organized the Metro Patriots—just being reassembled.

"Hi."

David looked up, shot her a smile, then returned to his work, remounting the slide to the frame.

"That young Lieutenant Wood is still out of it. Mildred gave him something to get his fever down and she has him on a course of antibiotics." She dropped down to kneel beside him as he began loading magazines for the pistol. "What's the plan?"

He didn't look at her as he answered. "We've got two high-priority jobs we have to get done. The logical thing is for you to run one of them and for me to run the other. You know those tunnels as well as I do. Which one you want?"

"You mean one of us checks out the lieutenant's story and then goes after rescuing these officers while the other one handles the raid on the Sheik Theater."

"Only way to get both jobs done in the time available. If the lieutenant's story is accurate, those officers he was with would eventually have to be killed. Makowski and Townes can't keep riding them around forever like that without the public getting wise. And their relatives and friends will eventually find a sympathetic enough ear in the press that the news will get out."

"Are you thinking the same thing I'm thinking?" Rose asked him.

He put a freshly loaded eight-round magazine up the well of the pistol and holstered the Desert Eagle in its SAS-style holster on the blanket near his right knee. "Yeah. I am, I guess. That the government, when they kill those officers, is going to try to pin it on us. Right now the Patriots are on an upswing since we got Rudolph Cerillia's taped broadcast where he named our self-styled President Makowski for being behind the real President's death. And our intelligence, as we both know, indicates troop movements toward several of the larger cities. That's going to take revolutionary spirit in the United States and turn it into all-out war. Unless Makowski can convince the general populace he's doing it to protect them.

"We know Makowski's linked to the FLNA," David went on. "And we know he's manipulated by the FLNA. But we don't know that he actually works for them. And even if he does, that's no guarantee the FLNA will take what happens to him into account when they make policy moves. That cease-fire the FLNA declared yesterday—let's say for a moment that it's even mildly legitimate, okay?"

Rose nodded, just watching his face.

David continued. "With no FLNA activity to speak of, what's Makowski's excuse going to be to keep troops in the cities? For the restriction of civil liberties? I mean, we know Makowski's trying to make himself dictator. But he can't just say that. He's got to have a reason.

"Kidnapping those officers and noncoms and then executing them and making it look like we're to blame," David concluded, "kills two birds with one stone for him. He gets potentially troublesome military leaders out of the way and provides the perfect excuse to occupy the cities so he can 'protect' the American people from us. If he makes it look convincing enough, a lot of people'll buy it."

"I'll take the tunnel job on the Sheik Theater," Rose told him. He reached into the side pocket of her field jacket for her cigarettes, took one, offered her one—she thought about what Mildred had said and shook her head—then lit it with her lighter. "You're smoking too much."

"You're right." David smiled. "Then you take the tunnels. Take Runningdeer and LeFleur with you and whoever else you need. I'll go after that train and take Steel and Blumenthal with me. Those FBI credentials of theirs might still convince somebody they're with the Bureau. This won't be a military operation unless it has to be, not until we know where and what the target is."

"All right. But what happens if Makowski moves troops into the city before we get out?"

"Then we're up that proverbial brown stinky creek without anything even remotely similar to a paddle."

Rose Shepherd decided to light a cigarette anyway.

Chapter Twenty-One

*T*hey were called cigarette boats because in the days when smuggling cigarettes was lucrative enough to be bothered with along the Florida coast, the small, fast speedboats were what was used. These days drugs were smuggled, and the boats used were large seaworthy craft with more sophisticated electronics aboard than a naval vessel, the best that unlimited money could buy.

And the cigarette boats were nearly loaded, some already starting north along the coast.

The load of guns, ammunition, and spare parts had been split nearly evenly among the cigarette boats and three small vans, all but one of these loaded and gone. Ashbrooke and two of the *Ruth II* 's complement helped now with loading into the back the last of the guns and ammunition taken from the dead drug dealers.

Kelly Martine was a pretty girl with long, whatever color she chose for the occasion, hair. Thomas Ashbrooke had known her father years before when he—Ashbrooke—had smuggled arms to anti-Batista rebels in the days when Castro was perceived as a liberator rather than a communist dictator. Ashbrooke had known her mother too. Her mother was dead and her father, these days one of many Cuban-Americans active in the Patriot movement, was leader of the Miami

Metro/Dade Patriot cell. She handed up the last two of the Uzi submachine guns and Ashbrooke slid them in place beneath a false panel. A cursory look by an inquisitive policeman or soldier at a roadblock would reveal nothing. But an experienced man would check for a false panel.

A cool breeze was coming in over the water, strong enough that it could still be felt well back from the beach in the trees near the side of the road where the trucks had loaded.

Kelly picked up her semiauto Uzi carbine and slung it to her shoulder. "So. Thanks for the stuff you got off those drug dealers, Mr. Ashbrooke. We'll be needing it."

Tom Ashbrooke knew that Patriots all over the United States needed arms, but he looked at her because of the odd inflection in her voice.

"Then you haven't heard?"

"What is it I haven't heard?" Ashbrooke asked her.

"Across the border with Mexico, to the Gulf Coast side of Florida, all along the Texas coast, in Louisiana and Mississippi and west from Texas—with the exception of Arizona—all the way to California. Infiltration. Heavily armed bands of men originating from Mexico where the government's already fallen to the FLNA. They've taken over a few small towns, letting things run as usual but keeping some government and police officials and prominent citizens as hostages, the people who won't go along with FLNA plans. It hasn't been cleared for dissemination to the public yet by Hobart Townes's office and it may not be for a long time because it's a clear-cut defeat for Makowski, but we have definitive word from Patriot cells in the affected areas. There've been some mysterious landings in the Gulf of Alaska too. There's a full-scale invasion starting but they're just sitting in place, like they're waiting for some sort of signal to get started, just massing more personnel and securing their own areas tight as a coffin lid."

"Holy shit" was all Thomas Ashbrooke could say for a moment.

"My father and some of the other Patriot cell leaders are trying to get the information out to the other cells as quickly as they can, but the information is so hot we can't trust regular channels. Your son-in-law, Dr. Holden, probably won't hear about it until the arms you brought in reach him. We wouldn't have known about it either except that when my dad was involved with the anti-Castro work he set up an information network all along the Gulf Coast and—"

"How'd he learn about the Alaska thing?" Ashbrooke interrupted.

"One of the guys he'd worked with during the Bay of Pigs invasion, a CIA case officer. The man just got disgusted with everything and quit the company and moved up north where he runs a flying service. He and Dad are good friends. He got word to Dad through a banker in Miami." She brushed her hair back from her face as the wind caught it.

Thomas Ashbrooke stared past her, toward the water beyond the beach. "I'll do everything possible to accelerate my shipping schedules. But once we run out of goodwill, we'll start needing money. You'll have to get your father to arrange a meeting—himself, some of the other Patriot leaders, like that—so we can work out a financial plan. I'm already getting some information put together on some likely revenue sources. But what's needed is for the Patriots to formally declare a government in opposition to the current government of the United States." Ashbrooke leaned against the back of the truck and lit a cigarette. "And before you say it, I know it's going to be tough. But otherwise we don't have a chance. If the FLNA has an invasion scheduled, we don't have a hell of a lot of time either."

"I'll tell my father and get him to pass the word up to Dr. Holden and to the other Patriot cells."

Ashbrooke nodded. "The meeting's going to have to be held in some safe spot overseas. We'll be needing your dad's help for setting that up. A lot of important people to smuggle out of the country and then smuggle back in. I'll put some people in touch with your father. He'll know them. They can work out the details. But this is going to have to be quick and the location for the meeting is going to have to be really closely guarded. I wouldn't put it past Makowski to invade a foreign nation just to get at the Patriot leadership."

Kelly nodded. "I'll tell him. You on your way back to the Bahamas?"

"Yeah, then to Israel. I can operate there a lot more freely. I've got a lot of favors still owed to me there and there's a lot of sympathy within the Israeli cabinet for the Patriots because Makowski's seen as a serious threat to stability in the Middle East."

Ashbrooke started walking with her toward the truck. The two men from the *Ruth II* were waiting by the water near the launch. When they reached the cab, she rolled back a floor mat and exposed a panel insert, then lifted it. There was a compartment inside containing spare magazines for the Uzi carbine, an oddly sturdy-looking knife, and a pistol along with about three hundred rounds of 9mm Parabellum ammunition.

"You tell your father thanks for his help." Ashbrooke extended his hand to her.

She took it, her handclasp firm and dry. "Dad told me to tell you he hasn't forgotten that time you saved his life in Cuba. Was that during the Bay of Pigs?"

Thomas Ashbrooke was almost embarrassed, shrugged, and figured she was a big girl. "No. It was in the Batista days and I was supposed to meet with antigovernment rebels. That was when the organized-crime people still owned casinos in Havana and the hotels and everything still got a good trade. Your father and this guy who looked like a refugee from a 1930s gangster movie started getting into it because of the way this guy was treating a woman at the bar. The guy pulled a knife on your dad and cut him a little—"

"That scar on the back of his hand?"

Ashbrooke nodded. "Yeah. That's the one. Your dad broke a bottle across the guy's face and put him down for the count. But then it turned out this guy was a big shot or something and three other guys came piling in, his bodyguards or something. The thing turned into a small riot.

"Anyway," Ashbrooke told her, "this one guy pulled a gun—only time anybody's ever shot at me with a .38 Super—and was just pulling the trigger on your father when I pushed him away."

"But you said he shot at you."

"Yeah, well, I pushed him away with my body." He was embarrassed now. "Don't think I was being that heroic. I miscalculated where the muzzle was going to end up. We got out of the bar, found the doctor the rebels were using, and both of us got patched up." There was a scar across his right rib cage from the bullet, but he didn't tell her that.

They walked around the front of the van and he helped her up behind the wheel. "You give your dad my best."

She leaned down and kissed him on the cheek.

Thomas Ashbrooke smiled, closed the door for her, walked back along the van's length, and secured the cargo door, then slapped his open palm against it.

As she pulled away, he thought he heard her shouting back to him, saying good-bye. He stood there, watching the van move along the two lanes of blacktop until it passed a bend and disappeared from sight. Then Ashbrooke started into the trees, toward the beach, toward the launch waiting for him there in the surf, toward the most difficult task that had ever faced him.

Without a government, the Patriots didn't have a prayer of being able to finance a war, of being perceived as anything but rebels by other nations of the world, despite the growing distrust within the global community for the intentions of Roman Makowski. But with a government— He recalled the words Julius Caesar uttered on one fateful day, as Caesar had recounted them in his chronicles.

Prepared to cross the Rubicon in defiance of his orders, he told those with him, *"Alea jacta est."*

The die is cast.

Chapter Twenty-Two

It was standard routine now for each Patriot cell to have within it a forger who, if he was lucky enough, could utilize actual government forms, if not re-create them, but however this person did it, manufacture identity papers. These were essential for any open movement within the cities, for travel along interstate-highway systems, for almost any activity when conflict had to be avoided in favor of anonymity.

Celine O'Brien was theirs.

David Holden looked over the twelve-year-old girl's shoulder. "You're very good," he told her.

"Thanks," she half mumbled.

Rosie looked at him, shaking her head, and Holden recalled his own daughters—dead now—and how easily little girls could become embarrassed. So he remained silent.

And after a while Celine began to speak. "We were low on those curfew passes. The last batch we got in, the printing was all fuzzy?" The way her voice rose at the end of her sentences reminded him of his daughter; some women never lost the habit. "But I put a couple of them away? Well, these are the best ones I've ever done."

Luther Steel picked up the curfew pass that bore his

photo, saying, "This looks like the genuine article, all right."

Celine smiled, saying, "Well, the passes are real, the laminating is real, and the photos are identical to the ones they really take when they give out the passes. And we use the same kind of typewriter. Only the numbers are wrong? You see, I don't have any way to get the numbers right because—well, there just isn't any way. The only way somebody could make this out as a fake curfew pass is if they recognized the number from another pass. It's the right series, the number, that is."

"These will be just great, Celine," Rosie told her.

David Holden spoke up. "I've got to ask you. How did you get so good? I mean, I've seen you duplicate letterheads by hand, uh—"

She looked embarrassed again. She was very pretty, with soft brown hair highlighted with strands the color of spun gold, her hair caught up at the crown of her head in a barrette. Her voice, normally alto, seemed a little deeper as she answered him. "I always wanted to be an artist. And when they killed—"

Rosie interrupted instantly. "How about those fake driver's licenses, Celine?"

Celine's face seemed to brighten as she opened the drawer of her modest desk and started to produce the documents. David Holden wondered how many other children would lose their parents before this was through. And he didn't want to know how many.

Holden stared at himself in the mirror. He wished that he could say that if he didn't know it was his own face staring back at him, he wouldn't have recognized it. But the modest changes in his physical appearance weren't that good.

His normally dark brown hair was dyed dark blond

with the kind of dye—it came in a pink plastic squeeze bottle—that would shampoo out but not wash out if it rained. Naturally wavy—he'd never liked that about his hair but his wife Elizabeth had always liked it and Rosie seemed to like it too—his hair was slicked back straight with mousse, without a part. The fake mustache, darker than his altered hair and lighter than his untouched eyebrows, was a good one, theatrical quality, and able to stand close scrutiny without looking faked—he hoped.

With a dark blue suit, an attaché case with faked but genuine-looking documents showing him to be an important businessman and the identity papers and credit cards (they had an imprinter that produced fakes that would have been good enough to use anywhere), he might just pass. He hoped.

Holden straightened his tie and started from the tent.

Outside, the afternoon was cool, and although the season wasn't yet far enough advanced for snow, the clouds coming over the mountains to the west seemed heavy-laden and gray and there was a bite in the wind.

When he reached the car, the first one there, he set down the attaché case and the bag containing his weapons and pulled on the lined khaki raincoat. There was a Patriot sympathizer in Metro who, before the troubles had started, had run a successful chain of discount-clothing stores specializing in men's and women's attire. Since the economic hardships, he was down to two stores and struggling to hold on to those, but no request made to him for help was ever denied.

Everything Holden wore, except for the knit tie, his socks and underpants and the fake mustache were courtesy of their friend, Mr. Rosenblum.

Rosie was coming across the camp as Holden looked toward the command tent. Like him, she was in civilian attire. Her operation to penetrate the Sheik Theater depended on successful infiltration of Metro as well. But they would leave for the city separately.

As she neared—there had been too much to do for them to spend much time together in the last hours—Holden saw her in greater detail and had to smile. "When's it due?"

"Knock it off, David. You'd better hope there isn't one due!" She came into his arms and Holden kissed her lightly on the mouth, then patted the swollen abdomen beneath her clothes. "Just don't say a word. Most people are still inclined to give a pregnant lady the benefit of the doubt." And she stroked her own abdomen gently, looking up at him and smiling. It was odd, seeing her with blond hair and brown eyes—a wig and contact lenses—and even odder thinking of her as pregnant.

When this ended, if they lived through it, he'd planned on marrying her, having children with her. They'd even talked about it. But if by some accident she became pregnant now, he would lose his best comrade-in-arms. The thought chilled him. "What've you got under there?" Holden asked her, forcing a smile.

"Wouldn't you like to know." She laughed. "Well, since you're the father, I guess you've got rights. Our little one's a Glock. My .45 was too heavy. It's getting packed away."

Holden just held her tightly to him. He wanted to tell her not to die, not to get hurt, not to take any of the chances that he knew she'd take if she had to.

Instead of any of that, David Holden told her, "I love you, Rosie." And despite the fact half the Patriots in the camp could have seen them, he kissed her so hard on the mouth that his lips hurt.

Chapter Twenty-Three

David Holden leaned his head back against the seat rest and closed his eyes, listening to the hum of the Chevy's little six-cylinder engine.

The last roadblock before entering Metro.

There had been something in the PSF man's eyes—not just the evil, but as if he knew something hidden, could look inside a person and know his secrets—and whatever it was in the man's eyes, Holden had been frightened.

As a SEAL team leader, he'd learned, and in later years relearned, that bravery had nothing to do with a lack of fear. The only persons who were fearless were insane. Conquering fear was the bravest act, everything else beyond that wall within oneself simple by comparison.

The PSF man had checked his papers, Luther Steel's, and Tom LeFleur's papers, then rechecked them. Then he'd asked them—with icy politeness—to step out of the car and well away from it. The wanding had come, like the things used at airports.

There was a bleep when the wand was passed beside Tom LeFleur's left rib cage, and for an instant Holden was seized with the fear that LeFleur had some sort of weapon on him. But the cause of the bleep, after

LeFleur had been ordered to turn his pockets out into a tray, was merely a ballpoint pen.

The car had been thoroughly searched but, thank God, not thoroughly enough. The weapons hidden within it—the car having been specially prepared by Mitch Diamond's people—were not discovered. The PSF man told them thanks and to have a safe drive and they climbed back into the Chevy and LeFleur pulled slowly past the roadblock and, in the sideview mirror, David Holden could see the PSF man looking after them, not at the pickup truck behind them.

Holden felt motion beyond the normal and opened his eyes. It was almost fully dark now, a light mist falling, the windshield wipers, on some intermittent cycle, brushing it away, but the few remaining functional streetlights haloed yellow in it. LeFleur was turning into the parking lot where they would rendezvous with the Patriots within Metro itself who would aid them.

This separate Patriot organization had come about out of necessity. Entering and leaving Metro was slow and dangerous, the risk of discovery considerable. Hence, a separate wing of the Metro Patriots who never functioned outside the city, only within.

This Patriot subcell was largely composed of women, factory and office workers, nurses, and teachers. The few men counted within its ranks were those too old or too young or too infirm to join the regular Metro Patriots and live outside the city.

From the backseat, Luther Steel said, "We're running a little late, I think. That blasted PSF man at the roadblock—this is like living in some communist country."

Holden, sitting fully erect now, his eyes scanning the parking lot for signs of trouble, answered, "I was thinking more of the Nazis, really. The PSF, to me at least, is more reminiscent of the SS or Gestapo, maybe a little of each. I wonder if he looks at everybody like that."

"Who?" LeFleur said, cutting the wheel left and pulling up in front of what was once a discount store, empty now, a sign proclaiming that it was for sale or for rent, the sign vandalized, dominating the boarded-up main-window section.

"That guy at the last roadblock," Holden answered LeFleur.

"He's a cocksucker, that's all. It was written all over his face," LeFleur declared.

"Well, regardless of his sexual preferences," Steel interjected, "he was scary."

"I'm glad it wasn't just me," Holden joked, not feeling at all amused. "I think we were looking at the future of the United States if the bad guys win, gentlemen."

"Don't even think that," Steel almost whispered.

"What? The future of the United States or that they'll win?"

"Either," Steel said.

LeFleur laughed a little and Holden looked at him. "What's so funny?"

"Well, we'll win, I mean, won't we?"

David Holden let out a long exhalation. He lit a cigarette, for once having remembered to take some of his own rather than rely on mooching from Rosie. "I'm a firm believer in the idea that the good guys always win. But then one comes to the definition of *win*. Is it a moral victory or a tangible physical victory? What if winning takes a century or a millenium? What if winning just means that when we die, for some reason God is generous and takes us into heaven and the bad guys, when they die, just rot in hell? What's winning?"

LeFleur didn't answer.

Steel seemed about to speak, but when Holden saw the van pulling into the far side of the parking lot he cut Steel off and said, "We've got company."

Chapter Twenty-Four

When she stepped out of the car she remembered to massage her fingers against the small of her back and draw her shoulders rearward, in case anyone was watching her and expected a pregnant woman to do that after having exited a vehicle. Bill Runningdeer was still holding the car door open for her and she smiled at Bill, saying under her breath, "These shoes are killing me!"

Runningdeer smiled back. "Your shoes are killing me too. You're standing on my damn foot."

She looked down. He was right. She stepped back and away and he closed the door.

What with the too-tight shoes—Mr. Rosenblum hadn't had anything in her size and these were a half size too short—and the padding against her abdomen under the damned girdle that was making her sweat and the wig that itched and too much makeup, Rose Shepherd resolved then and there that the next time she had to enter Metro surreptitiously, she'd think of something else. She could dress up like a bag lady and at least then she'd get to wear comfortable old shoes; but bag ladies didn't travel that much, so that might arouse suspicion and she'd still need a wig, since she wouldn't do to her own hair what she'd need to do to look like one.

"Shit."

"What'd you say?" Bill Runningdeer asked her.

"Never mind. A man'd never understand." She started toward the door of the garage, her right hand massaging her faked abdomen, her fingers as close to the Glock hidden inside the foam rubber as she could get.

She'd practiced drawing. Drop the purse, then whip up the front of the blue maternity top with the little white dots and tear open the Velcro.

It wasn't very fast.

She rang the doorbell beside the double doors, leaned back, and in the light of a bare bulb, read the sign: "ACME GARAGE." She just shook her head.

"Is anyone answering, sweetie pie?"

She looked back at Bill. "No—snookums."

Rose Shepherd rang the bell again.

This time the walk-through door inset on the right-hand garage door opened a crack and a flashlight shone into her face. "We're closed."

David was working on a set of universal recognition signs within the Patriots with the help of one of the men who was a Mason, but they still relied on code phrases or whistling some old tune these days. She licked her lips and started her rendition of "The Ballad of Paladin" from the milestone television adult Western of decades back.

The flashlight clicked off and whoever it was behind the door said, "Saturday nights, that and *Gunsmoke.*"

Rose Shepherd audibly sighed. But in case anyone was listening who shouldn't be, she quickly said, "Our car? That's my husband out there. We saw your garage."

"Well, I'll see what I can do," the man's voice came back. "Can he drive it in?"

"I think so. We were going to visit my mother," Rose

lied, summoning as much dramatic conviction as she could.

"Just a second, then come in."

Rose nodded, called to Bill, "Oh, Melvyn [the name on his fake driver's license], this nice man's going to help us."

"That's wonderful—"

And then Bill Runningdeer did something for which she would never forgive him. He called her by the name on her fake ID.

"—really wonderful, Sissy."

Chapter Twenty-Five

*T*hey'd followed the van for about half a mile and Holden's palms were sweating. There had only been a headlight-recognition signal and the van had pulled out, LeFleur driving out after it, deeper into the older section of Metro, farther and farther from any chance of making a break for it if somehow the Patriot wing within Metro had been infiltrated or crushed.

And this was a trap.

The van made a right—no signal, just the turn—into an alley.

"I don't like this, with the weapons stashed where we can't get at them," LeFleur hissed.

That was almost true.

Holden, in the front passenger seat, sat bolt upright and opened the glove compartment, reached up inside, and depressed the catch that prevented the box from falling all the way out when it was opened. He edged forward on the seat and reached down inside, his fingers against the flat surface that formed an artificial backing for the dashboard. He caught at the edge of it with his fingers and pulled. As he reached down farther, Holden's hand closed over the butt of the "community" .45. The personal weapons of each man were hidden in more inaccessible places within the vehicle, but this gun was specifically placed here to be accessible in an emergency.

David Holden hoped he was an alarmist. As he drew his hand out, his left palm closed over the top of the beat-up government model's slide and snapped it back, released it, let it fly forward.

Holden thumbed up the safety, keeping his thumb beneath it just in case, since they were in a moving vehicle and the car might be forced to stop at any moment.

He closed the glove compartment.

"That's just got Hardball in it, correct?" Steel asked.

"Yeah. It'll do the job if we have to, I hope," Holden answered.

The van they were following reached the end of the alley and turned right again, doubling back on its original direction. LeFleur made a fast stop, looked in both directions, and turned the Chevy after it. The street they were following now seemed to be at the edge of a warehouse district. Not a nice place under normal circumstances, Holden thought, not the sort of place where one would walk carefree even in the best of times.

"Is that van ever going to stop, or what," LeFleur stated rather than asked.

Neither Holden nor Steel answered him.

"Where's the ladies' room?"

The gruff-voiced, gray-looking man who'd let them into the garage—he was a Patriot sympathizer and she'd met his grandson, a Patriot cell member in Birmingham—jerked his thumb toward a partially open doorway at the far end of the garage.

"Thanks," Rose Shepherd told him, then started walking toward it. Bill, in coveralls taken from the trunk of the car, was underneath it on one of those sliding-board things, starting to free up their gear.

The closer Rose Shepherd got to the bathroom door, the more she realized it had been a mistake even to ask. She'd seen bathrooms that made her tell herself she didn't care if the whites of her eyes went yellow and her kidneys fell out. This couldn't be as—"Aww, shit," she said under her breath. There wasn't a toilet seat, to speak of. Instead of toilet paper, there was a stack of brown paper towels on the edge of the filthiest bathroom sink she'd ever seen.

She'd done it before. She'd do it again. When she got into the tunnels, she'd break off, find a quiet place and— She shuddered, turned, and walked back across the garage. "I just remembered something," she called out in a friendly voice to the gray-looking Patriot sympathizer.

"How come they sent a woman?"

She just looked at him. "Hmm?"

"How come this doctor guy, Holden, how come he sent you and this Indian?"

"A lot of us are coming for this, Mr. Wallace. There should be two more cars arriving here and we're using other entry points into the tunnels. This is going to be a good-sized force."

"What are you, then, a nurse, case somebody gets wounded?"

Rose Shepherd had to think about that for a second before she answered. "No. I'm in charge of the operation."

"A woman?"

"What?"

"They put a woman in charge of a thing like this? I can't believe it."

Rose Shepherd smiled. She reached up to her hair, told him, "I'm not really a woman. This is just a clever disguise." And she pulled off her wig and turned away.

Chapter Twenty-Six

*T*he older of the two men behind the bar—the place was one of those that had opened up after the over-the-counter sale of alcoholic beverages had been prohibited—dried an eight-ounce glass with a dingy-looking towel, the glass almost yellow-looking under the buzzing fluorescent lamps. The light reflected through his thinning hair off his balding pate.

Bars like this had sprung up all over the United States almost overnight. Liquor licenses—in some areas the bribery rates had to be enormously high because the profit potential was so great to liquor-license holders—could still be granted legally, but liquor stores were closed. So people came into the bars and drank instead of drinking at home, or came into the bars with Thermos jugs, old milk cartons, every sort of container imaginable and bought liquor by the glassful and took it home. This was illegal, but the business was lucrative enough that bribery likely figured in again.

There was a shortage of containers of all types, because glass containers other than drinking glasses were prohibited for sale, since bottles that were capable of shattering on impact against a solid object made too useful a tool to a rioter and were ideal in the construction of Molotov cocktails. Containers of all types—but this was the first time he'd ever seen anyone bring a baby bottle into a bar anywhere in the world.

The woman who'd brought in the little glass nipple-topped bottles stood before the bar, nursing a beer, while the second man behind the bar—younger than the one who was still polishing the same glass—filled the bottles a shot at a time with something out of a brand-name bourbon bottle that hadn't tasted like what the label said it was when Linda had tried it, offered some to Kearney, and Kearney had sipped it for himself.

A sip was all he planned to take. And he counseled Linda to do the same.

The man polishing the glass was staring at Linda Effingham again. "I don't like the way he's looking at me, Geoff," she whispered.

Kearney said nothing. There had been a choice, of course, bringing Linda inside the bar or leaving her alone in the woods while he went in on his own.

His eyes drifted back to the woman having the baby bottles filled for her. As each one was filled the barman took up a pencil and made a mark on a piece of paper then handed her the bottle. She took each bottle in turn —there were eight of them in all—and placed them inside a padded bag. As she would move the bag Kearney could just faintly hear the bottles clinking together as if some group of elves had stolen into the bag and were toasting their good fortune at finding something alcoholic to imbibe.

The last of the baby bottles was filled. Kearney picked up his glass and pretended to sip at it. The smell of what was passed off as whiskey here—Scotch, as the Americans called it—was positively vile and enough to turn the least sober person conceivable still possessed of any olfactory sense to teetotaling.

The woman took longer swallows of her beer.

Geoffrey Kearney lit a cigarette in the blue-yellow flame of his Zippo wind lighter.

In the streaky mirror behind the bar, he could also watch the main entrance to the basement barroom. And through that entrance now Kearney saw three men coming. One of them he recognized, the man whom earlier that day Kearney had spoken with, asking as laterally as he could for some action that would bring him money.

In the mirror Kearney saw the man—tall, redheaded, and freckle-faced like a man-sized Howdy Doody—turning to stare at him. "This may be an accident or it may be something else," Kearney whispered over the whiskey glass he'd raised to his lips, his voice low so only Linda would hear him, his lips barely moving. "That back door I pointed out. Be ready to move to it when I say, whether I'm with you or not."

"No."

"Yes, dammit," Kearney said more strongly.

"Hey! Borden!"

It took Geoffrey Kearney a split second to remember that Thad Borden was him this time around. "Hi—Bill, right? Shit, huh!" Kearney stood up and, as the tall red-haired man crossed the room and extended his hand, Kearney took it. "Wanna drink?" Kearney could reach the 5906 that was stuffed into his waistband at the small of his back with either hand, so the handshake was only moderately dangerous.

Thad Borden was, in the vernacular, a badass, and Kearney had to play that to the hilt if he wanted to get anywhere near the FLNA.

"Naw, listen. But I tell ya— Hey, whoa!" And Bill looked past Kearney toward Linda Effingham. If eyes had teeth, Linda would have been bitten. "This your squeeze, man?"

Kearney stepped aside, grabbing Linda a little

roughly across her shoulders. "Damn right. Don't even think about gettin' any of this, man." Kearney grinned good-naturedly.

Incredibly, Bill actually punched him in the right bicep—good-naturedly—and laughed. "We got a party goin'. You want some action, gonna be some action people there."

Kearney had been hanging around the bar for exactly this opportunity, but he couldn't appear too eager. "Hey, man, I dunno. The lady and me, we been on the road for a while, huh. You know how it is."

"Could use you a party, then!"

Kearney looked at Linda. She was smiling valiantly, but he knew the nuances of her expressions well enough by now to read her discomfort like a book for the visually impaired.

"Yeah, hey, why not?" Kearney grinned. He stubbed out his cigarette.

Linda giggled. "Yeah."

"See ya outside—"

"Hey," Kearney interjected, laughing a little. "You're not pickin' up booze from this place, huh? Tastes like cow piss."

Bill punched him in the arm again, annoying but something Kearney supposed was Bill's way of being manly. "Hey, no shit. Naw—we got good stuff. Man behind the bar caused me and my friends some trouble. Want in on payin' him back?"

Kearney had been noticing the other two men blocking the front and back exits. And now he noticed the woman with the baby bottles. She looked nervous, agitated.

And the man behind the bar who had been alternating polishing that same glass and visually undressing Linda Effingham was frozen as stock-still as if he were made of marble.

"Him?" Kearney asked.

"Yeah."

"What's in it for me?"

"We'll clean the till too, all right? You're cool for some money, huh?"

Kearney looked at Linda. She looked the part well enough, a little too much makeup, the clothes calculated for flash rather than style. He saw the hardness at the edges of her eyes, told her, "Wait here, kid." And he fell in beside Bill as the red-haired man sauntered toward the bar.

"Hey, Tommy, what's happenin'?"

The man buffing the glass, sweat in droplets around his eyes even though it wasn't hot in the bar at all, forced a grin. "Bill. I was lookin' for ya earlier today. I got that—"

"That was the money you owed us yesterday. Today it's twice as much."

"I don't—"

Bill was flipped over the bar and beside the cash register in the blink of an eye, shoving Tommy the barman back against his liquor display, the glass the man named Tommy had been polishing so assiduously falling from his hands, shattering on the slatted wooden floor. A bottle fell, but because the container was plastic all it did was bounce.

Kearney waited, not quite sure what he was supposed to do, but realizing something would be required of him because this was a test, and probably just a preliminary one.

Bill rang the register and the little minicomputer's drawer popped open. His hands scooped up the bills and two rolls of quarters, then he tore the money-slotted drawer out and flung it down to the floor behind the bar, coins rolling everywhere. Beneath the drawer was where in most registers the larger-denomination bills were kept. This register was no exception, three hundreds and a fistful of twenties.

Kearney determined that it was now or never, flipped up onto the bar and rolled down next to Bill. Kearney reached into the till and grabbed a second fistful of twenties. Bill looked at him, challenge in Bill's eyes.

"You said I could take part of the till, man, so I'm takin' it," Kearney said through his teeth.

Tommy, the barman, was moving. Kearney caught a flash of the man reaching under the bar at the far left edge of his peripheral vision.

As Tommy, a nightstick in his hand, wheeled toward them, Kearney had the gun out from under his jacket, the safety snapping up and off with a loud click. "Don't."

"Tommy, you—" Bill started, Kearney hearing the snicking sound of a switchblade opening.

Kearney, the Smith & Wesson in his left fist, straight-armed Tommy's chest with his right and sent the barman sprawling onto the floor. Kearney snarled, "You pull a club on me again, old man, and I'll shoot your ass." Kearney looked at Bill. Bill spat toward the barman and started to close his knife.

Geoffrey Kearney had just saved Tommy's life.

"Keep those twenties," Bill said good-naturedly.

"I was planning to," Kearney informed him and his eyes met Bill's eyes for a long second, then Bill laughed.

Chapter Twenty-Seven

*T*he van stopped.

David Holden moved his right thumb from beneath the old government model .45's safety to above it, ready to swipe it downward, the trigger finger of his right hand just outside the pistol's guard, ready.

The Chevy Tom LeFleur was chauffeuring stopped.

Luther Steel leaned forward. "Tom, you be ready to get this car out of here as quickly as possible."

Holden glanced over toward LeFleur. The ex-FBI man's right hand was on the selector. "You in neutral?"

"Sure am."

"Good. Luther, if we need them—"

"I know. Start ripping out the seat back so I can get into the compartment between the rear seat and the trunk."

"Right. Pop that pad over the dome light," Holden told him. But Steel was already doing it. The chrome-plated frame around the dome light was rigged to pull off instantly, beneath it Velcro fuzz framing the light. Steel pushed the pad in place, the Velcro hooks attaching to the pile. The other courtesy lights had been previously disabled.

Holden threw open the door.

Three women, one of them tall, were getting out of the van, the tall one walking toward the Chevy with her hand under her coat. For a gun? Likely. Holden knew very few of the Patriots working exclusively within Metro and this woman didn't look at all familiar.

Holden stepped out of the car, keeping his right hand with the .45 in it behind his right thigh.

As she approached he began whistling the recognition tune, "Ballad of Paladin."

The woman called back to him. "Saturday nights, like *Gunsmoke.*"

Holden breathed.

Chapter Twenty-Eight

Rose Shepherd turned a corner within the underground tunnel complex. It was private enough here.

The only sounds, aside from the rustling of her own clothes, were the drips from overhead. The tunnel system was something she'd always read about when she was a little girl, a part of Metro's history. Begun before World War Two as part of a massive subway-building effort, it had been abandoned when the war came and there were no materials for its completion. The subway system never resumed after the war. As a girl she had never dreamed she would be witness to people fighting and dying here.

In the early days of the fight against the Front for the Liberation of North America, FLNA forces had used the tunnels as their own private domain. It was a warren from which they could emerge anywhere within the inner city, from one of the numerous buildings whose subbasements were at the same level as the tunnels (punching through walls wasn't that difficult) or from beneath a manhole cover when a tunnel branch connected to the sewer system.

No one had followed them into the tunnels, attacked them where they were until the Patriots under Rufus

Burroughs had. And then David had led them back into the tunnels, after Rufus's death.

She remembered the little girl about to be raped by FLNA street punks, how David had saved her.

That little girl had somehow been a turning point for David, as much as the deaths of his family had been, as much as the death of Rufus Burroughs, whose Desert Eagle .44 David still wore.

It was the innocent who suffered the most in any war, and in a civil war—that's what this was, had always been—most of all.

She had the skirt and slip and maternity top stuffed into her pack, along with the foam-rubber pad that enhanced the look of pregnancy. As she began to dress—black T-shirt, black BDU pants, black field jacket with the American-flag patch of the Patriots sewn on the shoulder, combat boots—she wondered what would happen if somehow she did get pregnant. David made love to her frequently. She was one of those women lucky enough to be able to use the Pill without aggravating her thyroid or elevating her blood pressure or suffering from any of the common side effects.

But what if something went wrong?

She couldn't leave David to fight this war alone while she hid away in safety.

Rose Shepherd had seen the photograph of a statue once, its image—because she was a woman in a man's world and, worse yet, in a man's profession—sticking with her. The statue depicted the wife of the Italian revolutionary Garibaldi. Garibaldi's wife held a pistol in one hand and a baby, nursing at her breast, in the other. There were few heroic poses for women. The T & A movies with bikini-clad girls with unbelievably ample breasts jiggling in time to the automatic weapons they fired wasn't heroic, just stupid. But the photograph of that statue. That was heroic, heroic and very womanly at the same time.

"Bad for the kid's ears," she said under her breath as she buckled on her pistol belt.

Chapter Twenty-Nine

"The train stopped over there," and she handed him her binoculars, unraveling the neck strap from her long, dark brown hair. Holden took the glasses, grunted a thanks, and refocused them to stare down into the extremely well-lit train yard. "PSF trains come through there all the time. This is as close as we can get because it's heavy down there."

David Holden wasn't sure exactly what Julie Leer meant by *heavy*, but he got the general idea. They'd climbed the water tower in the abandoned industrial park, Holden wearing coveralls taken from the trunk of the Chevy to protect the blue suit that went with his disguise. From the catwalk surrounding the old structure, the entire railroad yard was visible. With the binoculars, he scanned toward both sides, on one side seeing a canal, likely the one Mitch Diamond had told them the injured young lieutenant had swum across with the ill-fated female officer. There was a parking lot beyond the canal, where they'd stolen the car they'd escaped with.

"If you're observing the trains, Julie," Holden began, "how come none of your people saw the officers being off-loaded here?"

"The man who was on duty up in the tower here yesterday morning was arrested yesterday afternoon.

The PSF took him for questioning—they're gonna torture the hell out of him and we can't do a damn thing—took him down to the horror show."

"The horror show?" Holden repeated.

"The old Sheik Theater. Nobody can get in there."

David Holden hoped very sincerely that she was wrong. "Let's move out." They crept back along the catwalk, Holden following Julie Leer until they were on the far side of the water-tower superstructure where they could stand without risk of observation from the train yard.

They looked at each other, dead level in the eye because of her height. "I want you to get all of your people on this. To find out where that train might have gone, if there are any other trains like it they've seen. Anything you can find out about it."

"This must be pretty important."

David Holden nodded, grabbed the handholds for the access ladder, and swung out onto it. He went down a step, looked up at her. "If we can rescue those officers and senior noncoms and get them into our corner against Makowski and Townes, it could just make the difference between winning this war and losing it. So, yeah, it's pretty important," Holden told her.

He started down the ladder and Julie Leer swung onto it after him.

Chapter Thirty

*T*he M-16 was slung across Rose Shepherd's back, the 9mm semiautomatic Uzi carbine in her hands as they turned the bend into the next segment of tunnel. "Let's stop here," she ordered sotto voce, Bill Runningdeer behind her passing the word along to the fifteen others of the group, Randy Blumenthal, the other FBI agent, among them. The assault force was entirely made up of Patriots from their own cell, none of the personnel—all of them men, besides herself—from the wing within Metro itself. The Patriots who operated solely within Metro just didn't have the experience, and this was one of those jobs for experienced people only.

The sixteen of them, counting herself and Bill Runningdeer, had infiltrated Metro in groups of two, parking their vehicles at various destinations providing easy access into the tunnel system, then rendezvoused at pickup points along the route to the Sheik Theater.

With her Mini Maglite clamped tight in her teeth and the map in her left hand, crouched with Bill Runningdeer and Randy Blumenthal flanking her so the light could not be easily seen by anyone farther ahead or farther back in the tunnel system, she checked their route. As best she could tell (because the map wasn't one hundred percent to scale), about a mile's march remained until they hit the main branch, then a half mile until they found the antechamber leading up to the Sheik Theater's basement, where the prisoners were kept.

In the days when the subway system was first being built, the Sheik had not only been Metro's most fashionable motion-picture house—Gable flicks, Bogie, and Cagney, all the greats—but a center for live theater as well, famous singers, tap dancers, the big bands all playing there.

As a showcase for the new subway project, the first station for the system—as it turned out, the only one— was built beneath the Sheik, a champagne supper held there while name talent entertained the rich and politically powerful.

What condition the subway station might have survived in was anybody's guess now.

But it was the way into the Sheik, to reach the objective.

"All right. We're getting close, guys," Rose Shepherd announced in a loud stage whisper, killing the little purse/pocket flash, taking the full-sized Maglite from her belt. It was the same flashlight she'd used as a cop, for everything from lighting her way to bopping bad guys. Around its head was a cylindrical shield so the beam could not be seen at any great distance. Each of them had a flashlight similarly modified. It was the only way to see in the tunnels.

By that light alone, they kept moving.

Chapter Thirty-One

It was like something out of a movie, at the beach house to which Kearney and Linda Effingham followed the red-haired man, Bill, one of those movies set in a postapocalyptic age where lawlessness and violence are everywhere and the Darwinian scenario for survival of the fittest translates into survival of the most bloodthirsty. Kearney parked the Suburban near a low dune, backed into the spot, moving the Suburban's massive tires back and forth over the sand to pack it down for better traction just in case they needed it. With the dune to the vehicle's rear, and the tight confines—a copse of pines—just ahead of them, short of a motorcycle, nothing could park and block them. And the Suburban was big and powerful enough to bowl over anything small.

"Now, I'm going to tell you this once. Stick right by me. If you have to go the bathroom or something, make sure I'm outside the door. If I tell you to do something don't ask questions, because there may not be the time for any answers. Clear?"

"You sound worried," Linda barely whispered.

"Look out there," Kearney told her, exhaling slowly.

A male and a female—the woman was barely in her teens, it seemed—were having sex in the backseat of a convertible two cars away. A dozen motorcycles were parked beside the pool, two men in sleeveless leather vests fighting drunkenly, a half-dozen men and women, similarly attired in jeans and denim, laughing, egging them on. Beyond the pool, another half-dozen people, mostly men, were congregated before a fence, bottles ranked on it, pistol shots echoing in the night as, drunkenly, they attempted, mostly missing, to shoot the bottles.

"That is what worries me," Kearney said definitively. He was heavily armed, the B&D Fazendeiro rubber banded up his right sleeve beneath the goatskin A-2 bomber jacket, the 5906 in the small of his back, the Cold Steel push dagger clipped into his sock on his left leg. "Alcoholic idiot punks like those are what the liberal establishment loved so much to point to, in your country and mine, when they were disarming us. Fools! Come on. And stick close." Kearney popped the lock switch, stepped out, hissing to Linda under his breath, "Remember? I'm supposed to be a punk too. Get your own door." He set the lock switch and the alarm and closed the door, the keys going into the side pocket of his black jeans.

Music, too loud, somewhat unpleasant because of the volume, blared across the night, the smell of sea air from just beyond the house mixed with the smell of alcohol and marijuana. As Linda crossed in front of the car and joined him, he cautioned her, "Bottle beer only, nothing that's easily tampered with or comes in a glass, right?"

"All right."

They walked across the sand, the breeze stiffening, the noise of the gunshots from the area near the fence louder, the laughter of the two idiots in the slugfest beside the pool almost lost beneath it all.

Bill, the red-haired man, had parked his car nearer to the house, his two cronies from the bar standing beside the car with him, all three of them lighting cigarettes. Kearney lit one as well, cupping his hands around the Zippo's chimney.

"That's some big mother you got there, man," and Bill pointed toward Kearney's car.

"That 454 hauls ass when I want it to, no shit," Kearney offered. He was getting tired of American accents. American speech could be quite pleasant, but some varieties, such as this one, fell as hard on the ear as some of the dialects of his own country.

He grabbed Linda roughly about the shoulders and, in tow with Bill and his cronies, started toward the pool area.

"Good waste of ammo," Kearney observed as the next pistol shot rang out.

"Harv, man, his brain's fried, but he's fuckin' good in a fight." Bill laughed.

Somehow Kearney had guessed the first part.

The upstairs bedroom of the small house on the fringe of the city limits was a perfect place to be trapped like fish in a barrel, but while the Patriots working within Metro were attempting to come up with a lead on the train, there was no sensible alternative but to hide out.

The television was on, a news special on the cease-fire declared by the FLNA while negotiations continued with the Makowski administration to bring about peace talks. Either the stale air in the house or the content of the program—likely a little of each—was making David Holden vaguely nauseated.

The knock on the door registered, but not fast enough before the door began to open.

As Julie came through the doorway Holden twisted toward the sound without thinking, just reacting, the .45 coming into his right hand, the sound of LeFleur racking the borrowed Mossberg pump in the next instant.

"Easy," Steel said, lowering the revolver, also borrowed, that was on line in a point-shoulder position with her pretty head.

"I don't have any information on that train you were interested in," she began, sitting down in a vacant chair, crossing her very long legs. "But I do have something maybe we should follow up: another train just like it could have the same kind of cargo."

Holden was already standing. He stayed on his feet. "Where?"

"In that same train yard. Right now."

Holden looked at Steel, then at LeFleur.

He let go a long breath, looking back at Julie Leer. "How many of the enemy and how many people can you round up?"

"At least three dozen PSF troops. There's the two women who were with me tonight and about six or seven others. On such short notice that's all I can get. We've all got guns and some ammunition."

Holden looked at the pump shotgun LeFleur still held. It was a good gun, but only a twenty-gauge. The revolver Steel had just set down on the table was a Smith & Wesson Model 63, the stainless version of the .22 Kit gun.

Low-power weapons in largely inexperienced hands —as shooters, the Patriot wing within Metro would be experienced enough, but as combat troops their experience was practically nil.

"We don't have any choice," Holden told her. "Get who you can. And fast."

He looked at Steel and LeFleur. "Time to get our stuff out of the car, gentlemen," Holden told them.

* * *

Holden had given the old .45 and its three spare magazines of Hardball to Julie Leer.

The television still blaring its news special about peace being at hand, Holden buckled on his weapons.

The shoulder rig with the smaller of his two double-column magazine Berettas, the 92F Compact, and the inverted sheath for the Crain Defender knife positioned behind the offside case for two twenty-round 93R machine pistol magazines—he slung the harness across his shoulders.

He picked up the Desert Eagle and its Southwind Sanctions holster, affixing the drop shank to the web belt of his BDU pants and closing the Fastex buckle. He closed the upper-thigh strap around his leg, securing the Velcro band, then repeated the process for the second thigh strap.

Holden picked up the black web pistol belt, securing it at his waist, the full-sized Beretta 92F in the Bianchi UM-84 holster in a cross-draw position near his left hipbone where he could get at the gun with either hand if necessary. Besides the holster, the belt was fitted with two double magazine pouches for the Beretta pistols, these magazines fifteen-round capacity, the cases identical to the two already positioned in the small of his back, except that these attached with Bianchi fasteners rather than fabric belt loops.

There were other items on the pistol belt, two of these hook-and-pile flap-closure pouches of identical construction, one of these carrying the B&D Fazendeiro lock-blade folding knife the pouch was designed for, the second carrying the larger of his two Mini Maglites, the AA-sized. The smaller Maglite was clipped into the left breast pocket of his BDU blouse.

An additional single magazine pouch was on his

pants belt, carrying the second eight-round spare magazine for the Desert Eagle .44.

Holden took up the musette-style magazine case for the M-16 on the table beside him, slung the case cross-body, right shoulder to left hip.

Holden slung his gas-mask bag into position, right to left like the magazine case, securing the chest strap. He opened the bag, giving a quick visual inspection to the M-17. The cheek-mounted receptacles carried general purpose/antinuclear filters. Holden rebagged the mask.

His body weight was slightly off balance, but that corrected itself with the addition of a rifle on his right side.

He picked up the M-16. For storage in the confined space of the vehicle, the hinge pin that attached the upper receiver and barrel to the lower receiver and butt-stock had been removed. He reassembled the rifle, cycling the action several times, snapping it off, then putting a thirty-round magazine up the well, slapping it home.

There was no reason to sling the rifle on, because they would be traveling by van to the railroad yard after exiting the building through the kitchen into the attached garage.

Holden turned to face Steel and LeFleur. Like him, they were suited up. No one was ever ready for something like this. "Let's go."

Chapter Thirty-Two

*T*he PSF used the tunnel system just as the FLNA had, or still did, to move from one section of Metro to the next without being discovered.

Rose Shepherd realized that almost too late.

"Back!" she hissed through her teeth to Bill Runningdeer. "Lights out!" A double column of men—she didn't know how deep—was moving along the tunnel segment into which she had just been about to turn.

And the PSF unit would have to come right at her and the seventeen other members of her assault unit.

There was no moving back along the tunnel, because the tunnel here was a straight shaft running back for some five hundred yards. To have taken that segment of tunnel in a dead run would have produced too much noise.

Time.

"Shit," Rose hissed under her breath.

There were niches in the tunnel walls for electrical panels that had never been installed, for other fixtures. "Pass it along, Bill," Rose Shepherd whispered into Runningdeer's left ear. "Up into those big cubbyholes in the tunnel walls. Be ready with knives if I give the word. Depends on how many. Or if they discover us. And no shooting. No noise. No lights except in the rear. Pass it on."

Rose Shepherd edged back largely by feel, and as she would pass one of the others of her assault force that she assumed Bill hadn't gotten to, passed along her orders.

The Patriots began disappearing from the faint, heavily diffused light of the two or three flashlights still in operation so they wouldn't trip over one another in total blackness.

Rose Shepherd found a niche in the wall, hoped there wasn't a rat living in it, couldn't climb up into it because it was too high. "Bill! Gimme a hand."

"It's me, Randy."

"Help me up."

Hands on her waist, one brushing against her left breast. "Sorry."

"That's okay, it was a wonderful experience." She was up. "I'm set. Take off, Randy." Maybe Randy was only a nickname? *Naw,* she told herself.

She unslung her M-16, drew the Big Ugly One knife she'd gotten from Kelly Martine, bunched her gloved fist around it.

In the darkness, after the scuffling of movement had subsided, the loudest thing she could hear was her heart beating, drumming insanely in her ears.

Chapter Thirty-Three

*D*avid Holden, Luther Steel, and Tom LeFleur crept along the embankment just below the level of the railroad yard, on their right side the canal. The water smelled.

Holden glanced behind them. Julie Leer and three other women, all of them moderately well armed in one manner or another, brought up the rear.

The four other women and one older man, all who could be rousted on such short notice from the ranks of the city wing of the Metro Patriots, were positioned strategically on the other side of the train, with the exception of the older man. In his seventies but not looking it, he claimed to be a crack shot with his deer rifle. The manner in which he spoke of his abilities, like the statement of fact rather than hollow boasting, gave Holden a measure of hope that the man was as good as he said. The rifle, a Browning BAR semiautomatic sporting rifle with a 3 × 9 power variable scope mounted to the receiver, was a .30–06, the granddaddy of all American game cartridges for the prolific array of loads offered for it—until Roman Makowski had made all of that illegal. During both world wars, it was the U.S. military cartridge.

If the man behind it had the abilities he credited himself with, Holden told himself that maybe they all had a slight chance.

David Holden signaled a halt, leaned back against the embankment, and cupped his hand around the head of the larger of his two flashlights so he could read the face of his watch. Rolexes—at least his—were luminous enough to see in heavy darkness but not luminous enough to read with accuracy in semidarkness. He read his now.

In about sixty seconds or less the four women should be in position on the other side of the train. Their tactical mission was to create a diversion, opening fire on the PSF unit, drawing the PSF away from the embankment and the canal beyond, then to scatter.

As Holden and the others attacked from what would then have become the PSF's rear, the old man on the catwalk of the water tower was to take out any heavy weapons with his deer rifle.

David Holden hoped.

He watched the black face of the Rolex a while longer under the concentrated beam of his flashlight. When he took the flashlight away, the luminous markings, having absorbed some light, were visible enough that he could watch as the dot on the second hand approached, then passed the twelve.

"Masks," Holden ordered.

At any moment—

Holden popped the cheeks on the M-17, the air foul and rubbery-tasting at first; but that would either pass or he'd no longer notice it, one way or the other.

Gunfire, sporadic at first, then concentrated, broke out from the area beyond the train.

Holden eyed the tower, as if he could see a bullet. But he could see the flash when it came. The old man would fire his first shot when the four women committed to the diversionary action began to break off and with-draw.

"Hope that old guy doesn't forget," LeFleur hissed through his teeth.

David Holden heard Luther Steel counter with, "Would you, Tom? Would you forget?"

Holden kept watching the tower catwalk.

LeFleur answered, "Don't mind me—this isn't like a bust. I'm nervous as hell. Heck, if I can still shoot when I'm that guy's age, it'll be terrific."

Holden still waited.

The shot came.

"Let's go!" David Holden shouted, to his feet, bolting up the incline of the embankment, the M-16, slung to his body, gripped only by his left hand at the front stock in a modified high port as he tore one of the AN-M8 smoke grenades from his web gear, flipping it over the horizon of the slope. Steel threw one of the same, as did LeFleur, Holden reaching for a second AN-M8.

As they hit the crest of the slope, smoke was every-where, good for up to two and one-half minutes, likely less considering the whisper of breeze that blew across the railroad yard. Holden flipped the second grenade, Steel and LeFleur tossing AN-M8s as well.

Holden glanced back once, the three women on the crest of the slope now, falling into prone positions with their rifles, the fire element for Holden, Steel, and LeFleur.

Holden brought the M-16 to his shoulder, fired a burst, getting two of the PSF personnel as they started to turn toward the smoke, killing them. Holden ran on, the train cars visible through the swirling smoke.

Holden thought he heard the shouts of men from in-side.

And then he heard gunfire from an unexpected direction—up. Holden shot a glance through the smoke toward the night sky. No lethal airborne surprises there.

His heart—if such were possible—felt as if it had stopped.

A half dozen of the PSF personnel on the roofs of two of the train cars, firing their M-16s down through the roofs.

One of the men took a hit that knocked his baseball cap off and punched a hole in his left temple. Holden glanced for an instant toward the water tower.

The old man there was as good as he'd said he was, his once civilian, legal, semiautomatic hunting rifle putting the PSF murderer down dead.

"The rail cars!" Holden shouted, running, firing a long burst from the M-16 into the center of mass of one of the PSF on the ground, bowling him back, the end of the burst catching the PSF man behind him in the side, knocking him down. Holden drew the full-sized Beretta from the cross draw–positioned holster at his belt, thumbed up the safety, and double-actioned a round into the PSF man's head.

Holden ran on toward the train cars, gunfire still pouring into the cars from the roofs. Another of the men atop the train cars went down dead.

Two for the old man.

A burst of automatic-weapons fire plowed the ground near Holden's feet and Holden backstepped, wheeling toward its origin, firing out the M-16 in his right hand and half the magazine from the Beretta 92F in his left, bringing down one man, wounding a second. Steel sprayed a burst from his M-16 into the wounded man—the man was still firing—and killed him.

Holden ran on toward the train cars. He safed the Beretta and stuffed it into his trouser band, dropping the spent magazine for the M-16 to the ground to police up afterward, ramming a fresh one from the bag at his left side up the well, cycling the top round into the chamber, firing a burst toward two PSF personnel trying to crawl under the train cars.

He killed one man, missing the second.

Tom LeFleur was just ahead of him, fire from the roof of the nearest of the boxcars bringing him down, LeFleur rolling, his left arm limp at his side, his left leg stiff as he came up firing an M-16 one-handed, killing one of the men on the roof of the nearest boxcar.

Holden hauled the M-16 to his shoulder, fired a long, ragged burst, killing another of the men atop the boxcar roofs. Something tore across Holden's right thigh and Holden fell, rolled onto his back, stabbed the M-16 toward the origin of the enemy fire—two PSF men taken cover between two of the boxcars—and fired. Answering fire plowed into the ground beside him, a bullet impacting the receiver of his M-16, the assault rifle torn from Holden's grip, his fingers and wrist stinging.

Holden's left hand found the butt of the 92F, fisted it. He fired, a double tap killing one of the men instantly, the PSF man's head snapping back, slamming against the side of the boxcar, the left eye a gaping hole, another hole in the thorax.

Holden rolled, firing the Beretta as he tried to find cover, more assault-rifle fire churning the ground around him. The full-sized Beretta was empty now.

Holden stuffed it into his waistband again, the slide still locked open, as he hit the embankment and went over it, spread-eagling his arms and legs to slow his fall. His right leg was stiffening from the back of the thigh outward. "Shit," Holden hissed.

His right hand was numb and he slapped it against his thigh, trying to restore feeling. The mutilated M-16 hung at his right side as he dragged himself up.

LeFleur and Steel were in trouble, Steel trying to drag LeFleur to cover.

Holden's right hand was starting to get feeling back into it but not enough, not yet.

With his left hand Holden reached to the smaller Beretta in the shoulder holster slung beneath his left arm, twisted his fingers, tore the 92F Compact from the leather and thumbed off the safety.

Two more PSF men joined the one still alive between the two boxcars.

Steadying the smaller Beretta over his right forearm, Holden fired once, then again and again and again, bringing one of the PSF men down.

Assault-rifle fire churned dirt and gravel near Holden's face as he rolled laterally and right. The angle was oblique to the target, but he steadied the pistol again, firing a fast double tape, catching a second PSF man at least once, spinning him back into the boxcar wall.

Holden reached to his web gear, his right hand stinging but almost normally responsive.

He grabbed for his last smoke grenade, tore it clear, and flung it toward the gap between the two boxcars. In the confined space, when the cannister detonated, smoke seemed almost instantly to engulf the wounded man and the other one.

Holden fired two more rounds from the little Beretta, then another two as he dragged himself to his feet. Since the right leg still worked despite the pain, it couldn't be too bad, he told himself.

His right fist closed painfully over the butt of the Desert Eagle. He fingered away the safety strap, drew the .44.

Limping as he ran, Holden started for the boxcars, firing out the last six rounds in the smaller Beretta as he reached the denser cloud of smoke between the cars, hearing a gasp of pain from within the cloud. He thrust the smaller Beretta into his waistband beside the larger one.

Steel and LeFleur, in the relative safety of cover below the crest of the drop, were firing toward the roofs of the boxcars.

Holden, still gripping the Desert Eagle, started up the ladder of the boxcar to his right, no way to tell if all resistance immediately near him had been crushed, but time running out for the men in the cars, if it hadn't already.

He neared the top of the car, swung out, clinging to the top rung with his left hand, his right leg swinging free.

As Holden peered over the roof of the car behind him, a PSF man with an M-16 that had been spraying down through the boxcar roof wheeled toward him.

"Die, motherfucker," David Holden rasped, the Desert Eagle .44 at the full extension of Holden's right arm as he squeezed the trigger, the ordinarily mild recoil of the heavy gas-operated semiautomatic sending a spasm of pain up Holden's wrist and along his forearm.

The single 180-grain Jacketed Hollow-Point bullet hit the PSF trooper at the bridge of the nose, his face distorting with it, the head snapping back, the body dragged after it, the M-16 spraying wildly skyward as Holden ducked.

Gunfire from the ground toward the roof. Holden swung out, looked, swung back. Steel was running toward the boxcars, LeFleur and at least one of the two women still giving fire support from the crest of the embankment.

Holden safed the Desert Eagle, dropped it into the Southwind Sanctions SAS holster on his right thigh, closed the safety strap.

He reached to his shoulder holster's double magazine pouch beneath his right arm, pulled out one of the twenty-round magazines for the Berettas. Thrusting the magazine into his waistband, he tugged out the larger of the two pistols, buttoned out the spent magazine, letting it drop because he'd run out of hands. He stabbed the pistol back into his belt, rammed the fresh twenty-round magazine up the well, redrew the pistol, thumbed down the slide stop, and left the hammer cocked.

He shouted, hoping Steel could hear him. "Now, Luther!"

Holden punched the 92F up over the roof of the boxcar to which he still clung, keeping his head down, turreting the 9mm right and left and right and left as he pumped the trigger as fast as his right first finger would move. He felt pain across the back of his hand.

Assault-rifle fire echoed from below him.

As he drew his hand back, there was blood across the knuckles.

A grazing wound, either a bullet or debris.

Holden stabbed the empty Beretta into his belt, redrew the Desert Eagle, and hauled himself up, rolling over onto the boxcar roof, slamming into the body of a dead PSF man.

Holden came up to his knees, his right thigh screaming at him with pain now, the Desert Eagle in both fists. A PSF trooper spun toward him, firing, the boxcar roof in front of Holden shredding as Holden fired the Desert Eagle, then fired it again, then again, the PSF man's body twitching left, then sprawling back, his rifle spraying outward over the side of the boxcar, his body tumbling over after it.

Holden dragged himself to his feet.

"Luther! We're clear!"

Holden turned, started to wave up toward the water tower.

He could make out the old man, standing there on the

catwalk, rifle over his head at the full extension of his right arm in a signal of victory.

There was no more gunfire.

David Holden tore off his gas mask.

Twenty-four men, but with the element of surprise, that made the odds not that terribly bad. If these twenty-four men were allowed to pass, escape from the Sheik Theater with the freed prisoners and the arms and ammunition stored there might be blocked.

Rose Shepherd's right fist tightened on the haft of the Big Ugly One.

"Get 'em," she said just above a whisper, hurtling her own body out of the pitch-black niche in which she'd been hiding into the fragmentary beams of yellow light from the flashlights in the hands of every other of the twenty-four PSF personnel.

Her body slammed into the back and shoulders of the man immediately below her, her knife stabbing into the right side of his neck, her eyes squinting against the blood spray as she turned her face away.

As he fell forward she rolled left and off, catching up his flashlight as she came down hard on her knees— what she didn't want to be when she got old was a retired freedom fighter with housemaid's knee. Her left hand grabbed for the dead man's flashlight as it rolled past. As she stood and another of the PSF personnel spun toward her, raising his M-16, Rose Shepherd backhanded him across the bridge of the nose with the head of the flashlight. He screamed, his face twisting away as her right arm arced forward and she thrust the Big Ugly One in beneath his solar plexus and upward, edge up, drew it out, stabbed it in again and killed him.

There were groans of pain and death from all around her in the darkness, flashlights rolling everywhere across the tunnel floor, crazily twitching beams of yellow casting shadows and gone.

A hand reached for her and she started to hack downward with the knife.

"Me, Rosie! Look out!"

She caught herself as she heard Runningdeer's voice, felt him push her back, saw the momentary silhouette of him raking a knife blade across someone's throat.

A rifle butt swung toward her and she ducked, dodging left, punching the knife in her hand outward in a purely defensive reaction, the flashlight in her left hand crashing downward, a sigh, the smell of fecal material as somebody's bowel muscles relaxed in death, pain in her wrist as the Big Ugly One's blade skittered over bone or hard muscle, a hand groping for her in the darkness, falling away.

There was no noise anymore.

Nothing. "Sing out if you've got a live one!"

Nothing.

"Everybody! Sound off fast!"

"Runningdeer!"

"Blumenthal!"

Eleven other names came back as Rose Shepherd turned the battered but still functional flashlight across the ground.

Twenty-four PSF personnel were dead or dying.

Two of her own people lay dead.

None of her people were wounded beyond light scratches.

She leaned back against the tunnel wall, her right fist so bunched on the haft of the knife she didn't know if she could open her fingers.

Steel helping him, Holden threw open the door of the first boxcar. Using an M-16 taken from one of the dead PSF personnel—despite the Patriots' shortage of weapons, it was the only thing available—as a pry bar, they'd broken the lock.

Julie was wounded. Three women in all were dead. LeFleur had two wounds, neither of them serious. Steel had cut his hand, but it seemed to have bled itself clean, and Julie had indicated earlier that one item of equipment the urban wing of the Metro Patriots did have available was a complete medical kit and there was a doctor available to help them with anything serious.

David Holden closed his eyes, vomit welling up in his throat.

Each man within this boxcar and the two others would be meticulously checked, but everyone here—the forty or so bodies heaped over one another, men clearly trying to save their comrades by shielding them with their own dying bodies—seemed dead.

Holden's leg hurt him very badly.

"Luther. Let's get the next boxcar opened."

Holden climbed down as carefully as he could, the pain in his leg worse because he had the time to be aware of it.

He gave up, walked over to the space between the cars, and threw up, then picked up the M-16 that they'd used as a pry bar so they could get to work on opening up the next boxcar. But David Holden was already convinced that what they would find there would be much the same.

Her right hand was still bunched into a fist and she made a conscious effort to flex her fingers.

With only one flashlight lit at the front of their column, in Runningdeer's hand, and one at the rear, their progress was piteously slow, but there was no choice.

They'd taken the usable gear and the weapons from the bodies of the dead PSF personnel, but weighted down with twenty-four additonal M-16s and twenty-four Beretta M9 pistols, plus attendant spare magazines, they would have made virtually no progress at all.

Instead Rose Shepherd made a command decision.

Detailing two of the total of thirteen Patriots under her, she went on with a force reduced to twelve, counting herself. The two left behind had three missions: first and foremost, because the living were of more importance than the dead, hike the bulk of the liberated PSF weapons to the exit point they would use when fleeing the tunnels; second, evacuate the bodies of the dead Patriots so these men would be assured a proper burial rather than something else she didn't want to think of; third, keep secure the segment of the tunnel complex through which the remainder of the force, as well as those persons able to be rescued from the Sheik Theater, would pass.

As she made it now, counting off paces, in a matter of moments they should reach the segment of the tunnel from which they would be able to enter the solitary subway station, beneath the Sheik Theater.

She tripped in the darkness, caught herself before she fell, and kept going.

All three cars were open now and, so far, only nine persons, one of them a woman marine, were even close to being alive.

They worked as quickly as possible because they were running out of time. LeFleur, unable to assist with moving the wounded, took command of their perimeter security while the van, two station wagons and two pickup trucks and the Chevy in which Holden, Steel, and LeFleur had originally entered Metro were loaded with the wounded.

Despite his own wound—it had been hastily bandaged to minimize additional blood loss and keep him from joining the wounded—Holden carried the injured female marine in his arms, toward the Chevy. Her wounds would not preclude her sitting up and, with space at a premium, that was an important consideration. There were at least two bullets in her left leg and she had a chest wound that was only a deep graze.

The latter wound was starting to bleed through as Holden set her into the front seat.

"Who—who are you?"

It was the first time she'd spoken. She was pretty, about twenty-eight, black.

"I'm the notorious David Holden. Don't think I'm trying to get familiar, but I've got to look at that chest wound."

"All right."

He folded back her uniform shirt. To access the wound originally, one of the women who'd first bandaged her had cut away much of the left cup of her bra. Holden, as gently as he could, his own right hand a little stiff from the light grazing wound he'd gotten on the top of the boxcar, tried to adjust the packing. The bullet wound had penetrated about a quarter inch or better across her left breast about two inches over the nipple.

"How—"

"Your breast should be fine. Maybe a little scar," he lied. The wound would probably leave a good-sized scar that would require plastic surgery to eventually do away with.

"No . . . the others in—"

"We have a number of men—you're the only woman —who survived, Captain. How long have you been a captain?"

He thought he'd hurt her, that she was sucking in her breath. But as he looked into her face he could see tears welling up in her eyes. "All of them?"

"That's right. Eight men and you, Captain."

Holden took a first-aid dressing from his own gear and applied it to the wound as packing.

"Six weeks."

"What?"

"Been a captain six weeks. Who—"

"The PSF, on Townes's orders, likely on Makowski's orders before that. Anybody say anything we could use that—"

"You're wanting to know about any others."

"That's right."

"Just that I heard somebody, some PSF officer, I heard him say . . . say that this was the smallest train."

"Shit," Holden murmured. Then, "Pardon me."

"Everybody said you and your Patriots were the bad guys."

Holden was nearly finished, looked at her, and smiled. "That's what they say. You figure it out, Captain. What's your first name?"

"Holly."

"I'm David. You'll be fine, Holly. Can you wait here on your own? We've got a couple more people to move off the train."

"Yes."

Holden put a blanket over her, tucked it in, smiled, and got up from the half-kneeling position he'd taken—his thigh hurt badly—and started to leave.

"David?"

Holden turned around, looking at her. "Holly?"

"I think you just made nine converts to your cause."

Holden smiled. "You just rest easy. We need healthy converts and the less you move, the less you'll bleed. Okay?"

"Yes, sir."

Holden shot her a salute. "Yes, ma'am."

Chapter Thirty-Four

*I*t was positively beautiful.

Rose Shepherd stood there and only realized she was still looking up at the intricate mosaics set into the ceiling of the Sheik Theater station when her neck started to get stiff.

There was light emanating from the height of the low, graceful steps leading upward from the station level where, Runningdeer and Blumenthal flanking her, she knelt in the darkness. But even in the much diffused yellow light, the ceiling was one of the most beautiful things she'd ever seen in her life.

It depicted the history of the Sheik Theater. That was obvious at first glance. Women in gorgeous long dresses and men holding tall silk hats stood before the theater entrance, on the marquee the name of some long-ago forgotten star. In the next panel women leaning gracefully forward from a box overlooking the stage, holding delicate binoculars before them in long-gloved hands, a man's animated gesturing in the foreground, in the background a rank of ballet dancers forming perfect ballet bubbles with their arms.

In the next panel—she stopped herself.

Rose Shepherd inhaled.

"Bill. Bring up the others, six of us on each side. If they don't have guards down here—and I don't see any cables for cameras—then they have guards at the head of the stairs."

"Right." And Runningdeer began edging back on knees and elbows.

Rose Shepherd took one more look at the ceiling. She'd have to use the explosives here as she'd intended.

She'd feel like a murderer.

Steel drove the Chevy. Holden, his suit jacket awkwardly pulled over his BDUs and his field jacket stuffed down onto the floor, sat in the backseat, an M-16 across his lap. LeFleur was stretched out across most of the seat, his injured leg propped up.

Holden's own right leg was hurting a lot less, but it was also stiffening. A deep grazing wound was all it was, or possibly a bullet fragmented after a ricochet had passed through the fleshy part just under his rear—Steel couldn't tell when he'd bandaged it, except that there was apparently no bullet inside.

David Holden looked at his watch.

As if Steel were reading his mind, Luther Steel asked him, "How's the schedule. Will we make it?"

"I don't know. Rosie should have started the attack by now, may even be into the withdrawal. If she was much ahead of her schedule, we'll never rendezvous with those trucks. If she's running a little late, we've got a chance."

"If we don't make it," LeFleur said, "we're out of luck getting out of Metro until tomorrow night and probably security will be tighter then, between us hitting the train yard and Rosie hitting the PSF at the Sheik."

"You've got it." And Holden looked at Holly, the marine captain, either asleep or passed out in the front seat. If they didn't make it out tonight, there was a substantial chance they'd never make it out alive.

Just before leaving camp for their phase of the penetration, Holden had received word from Mitch Diamond that the PSF, supported by a mixed force of regular army and presidentially mobilized national guard, were to enter the city just before dawn for full military occupation.

LeFleur and Steel both knew that too, but there was no sense reminding them.

David Holden lit a cigarette.

Chapter Thirty-Five

*R*eefer was a pimple-faced kid with an imitation Armani suit and a pearl-handled (likely J. Scott Grips) synthetic Colt government model sticking out of the narrow-belted trouser band. He looked vaguely like someone dressed up for Halloween as a pimp or a pusher.

"This is Thad Borden." Bill, the red-haired one with the lined face, concluded the introductions.

"Nice-looking piece of ass you got there, Thad. I been watching you guys." Reefer grinned, sticking out his right hand.

Geoffrey Kearney took it. He would have preferred to chop it off. "Hey, thanks, man. But you keep that in mind—she's mine," and Kearney laughed.

Reefer took a step back, started to reach for his pistol, and as Kearney started to react, Reefer started to belly laugh. "Hey! Hey! Easy, man!"

Kearney snapped his empty right hand forward, his first finger pointed at Reefer's chest. As Kearney lowered his thumb, he went, "Bang!"

"Yeah. Maybe like Bill says, maybe we'll talk."

"Mr. Johnson here yet, Reefer?"

Reefer looked to right and left, let his eyes twinkle a little, answered in a whisper, "Never goes noplace without me these days. Yeah. He's here. Upstairs with some of the big shots. Told me to watch everything down here." A pistol shot rang out from out by the pool. "And tell that motherfucker to stop shootin' his damn gun or I'll ram it up his ass."

Geoffrey Kearney brightened. He liked killing two birds with one stone. "Let me, man."

Reefer just looked at him. "You wanna kick ass with Harv?"

"I jus' wanna kick ass," Kearney told him. And then Kearney reached out, caught Linda by the wrist, and pulled her toward him. "Lin, baby. Meet Reefer. Reefer's important. He's gonna watch out for ya while I go make somethin' happen."

Linda's eyes flashed up at him. She forced a smile, then looked at Reefer. "Hi, Reefer."

"Hey, good-lookin'—whatchya say you and me watch your old man here try kickin' some ass."

Linda made herself laugh. "Whatever." She pushed her skirt down along her thighs with the palms of her hands, giggled realistically.

Kearney was beginning to think Linda Effingham should have been an actress.

Kearney heard another pistol shot and started across the beach house's living room, shouldering his way through the crowd, the smell of marijuana thick and sweet and heavy on the air. Kearney passed a coffee table and set down his glass of whiskey—Scotch, he reminded himself—and went through the open patio doorway onto the pool deck.

He could see Harv and three of his friends, more drunk than before, reloading.

There was a sea of broken glass in front of the fence.

Kearney looked back once, Reefer, with Linda in tow and red-haired Bill behind them, coming through the crowd toward the doors.

Taped rock music was playing too loudly, just like the way everybody was laughing.

Kearney skirted a couple grinding on each other on a bath towel at the edge of the pool, reached the deep-end side, and waited while Harv closed the cylinder on his revolver.

"Yo! Asshole!" Kearney called out. With the pool at his back—there was nobody swimming because the night air was too cold—no innocents would be in immediate danger if things got to shooting. He wasn't planning on settling it that way, but shooting was always possible if he couldn't manage the situation properly. Innocents. He doubted there was an innocent at the party, with the exception of Linda. In his own way, he was more like them than he was like her.

Innocence was something Geoffrey Kearney had lost a long time ago.

Harv turned around, stared at him drunkenly. "What you say?"

"I called ya an asshole, man. We're damn tired of this fuckin' wild-West show, so put the gun down."

The idea, of course, was to make himself look ridiculously tough by taking care of Harv and use that to pressure Reefer to introduce him to "Mr. Johnson," Dimitri Borsoi, if not the head then certainly one of the top men in the Front for the Liberation of North America, right here in this house.

"I should what?"

"Put the gun down before I put it where the sun don't shine."

Harv—he was taller than Kearney by a head at least and half again as broad in the shoulders and chest—looked at his revolver, then looked at Kearney. "You want some a this, badass?"

"If one or two more shots is what it takes to shut you up? Hell, yeah."

Kearney wasn't quite certain what would happen next. If Harv made to shoot, Kearney, with no gun drawn, would be at a distinct disadvantage. But there were ways of evening things up, if necessary.

Harv, instead of shooting, apparently wanted to talk some more and show himself as being the toughest thing on two legs. Leaving his cronies standing drunkenly near the fence, their guns in their hands, he started to walk—lurch might have been a better description—toward Kearney. "You gonna be dead, man."

"You talk big, Harv. But all you are is shit."

Harv kept coming, just a little faster.

Geoffrey Kearney had to be very careful. If he made this look too good, he might arouse suspicion, but it had to be good enough to keep him from getting killed.

Harv stopped walking, just stood there, about twelve feet away.

Geoffrey Kearney—slowly, so the action wouldn't be mistaken for something else—took out his cigarettes and his lighter, lit a cigarette, pocketed the pack and the Zippo. Where his left hand was now, he closed it over the butt of the 5906 very quickly.

Harv said something to his pals by the fence and they laughed.

Kearney studied the tip of his cigarette, then started walking toward Harv. "Guys like you gimme a pain, Harv. Know that? So I figure you hand over that gun, or I'll take it. You choose."

Harv's eyes hardened, the glassy look of drunkenness dissipating in an adrenaline rush. Harv would be aware of that, feel it, realize he should stall until the adrenaline took over.

Kearney walked closer, now about five feet from Harv. The closer Kearney got, the bigger Harv looked.

"You know, Harv, I was thinkin' maybe you gimme

the gun, I let ya walk, huh? But, naw, I'm gonna kick some ass. And it's gonna be you."

Kearney tugged at his left earlobe.

Harv started to react. Kearney saw the muscles in Harv's face tighten. Kearney snapped the cigarette out, right toward the center of that face. It didn't matter if he connected or not, because the natural reaction would be to close the eyes and turn the face away.

Harv reacted naturally.

Kearney took two long steps, as he did his left hand arcing outward and downward, the second and third fingers wedging outward into a V, closing over the gun-hand wrist and the rearmost portion of the revolver, the heel of Kearney's right hand smashing upward and outward, intentionally missing Harv's nose—a blow there with the force and direction Kearney was using would have killed instantly—impacting Harv's mouth just below the lower gums and above the point of the jaw, Kearney's right knee smashing up, Kearney's left hand already sweeping the gun away to Harv's left. Kearney wheeled half left, as he did bringing his right elbow up in a tight arc against the left flat of Harv's jaw. Kearney's right forearm crossed over his left hand, Kearney's right hand smothering the trigger guard and much of the forward portion of the revolver.

Kearney arced both his arms upward, dragging Harv's gun hand with him, snapping his arms down hard to the right, twisting the gun from Harv's fingers as Harv's gun-hand wrist and elbow almost simultaneously snapped. Kearney maintained the rotation of his right arm, the gun tearing away from Harv's fingers. Kearney took a half step back on his left foot, pushing the butt of Harv's revolver into his open left hand.

He had the muzzle trained on Harv's drunken pals as Harv's body collapsed at his feet. "No one moves!" Kearney hissed.

From behind him and to his left, he heard a voice.

Although he'd never heard it before, somehow he recognized it, knew how it would sound.

"Mr. Borden. I'm impressed. We should talk."

Geoffrey Kearney looked around.

Standing six feet away from Kearney, his hands empty, easy to kill in the blink of an eye, was Dimitri Borsoi, if not the leader then certainly one of the top men in the FLNA.

"My name is Johnson. I could really use a man like you, if you're interested."

Instead of pulling the trigger, Kearney grinned and said, "Yeah. Maybe I'm interested. What's in it for me?"

Borsoi grinned broadly and extended his right hand.

Kearney's right hand was a little bloody from Harv, but Borsoi clasped it anyway.

Chapter Thirty-Six

Charges were planted along both sides of the subway station and around the bases of each of the six ornate support pillars. As best she could tell, the pillars were not for decoration, but actually held up the roof—that pretty roof.

Rose Shepherd crouched at the base of the stairs, the light here still dim, she realized, so bright by comparison to the pitch-blackness of the tunnels that she squinted against it before bringing her goggles up from around her neck and over her eyes.

Randy Blumenthal, beside her now, was giving a last-minute check to the Hawk MM-1 grenade launcher, its charging holes loaded with sound-and-light grenades. An MM-1 was as useful to a commando as an electric can opener was to a cook, she thought, or maybe more useful, like a microwave oven that speeded things up.

"Ready when you say, Rosie," Blumenthal told her.

Rose Shepherd just nodded, the M-16 feeling heavy in her hands, as it always did until the fight started and suddenly it felt so light sometimes she would look down at it just to make sure she was still holding it. A second M-16, liberated from the bad guys they'd iced in the tunnels, was slung under her left armpit, chamber-loaded.

Bill Runningdeer was at the opposite side of the

stairs, five Patriots behind him, Bill's right hand holding his Uzi submachine gun, his left hand holding a SIG-Sauer P-226 with a twenty-round magazine in place. There was an M-16 across his back.

Slung across her back was the full-sized Uzi semiautomatic carbine she'd gotten from Kelly Martine at the same time she'd gotten the knife—the Big Ugly One—that she'd used in the tunnels.

She didn't want to think about that. She'd killed with a knife before and she'd kill with one again, she realized, but it was never something she ever wanted to think about. When she got to the point where thinking about killing long enough didn't make her want to throw up, it'd be time to quit, war or no war.

Because she would have become the enemy herself then.

Behind schedule because of the twenty-four PSF men in the tunnel and the necessity of the ambush, she didn't bother looking at the Timex Ironman on her left wrist.

She just raised up from her crouch, gave Bill a silent hand signal, and started up the stairs.

Holden finished reloading the 92F Beretta magazine that circumstances had forced him to drop when he'd been working to knock out the PSF personnel atop the boxcars.

The Chevy was turning a corner as Holden looked up.

The trucks were still there. Rosie hadn't escaped the tunnels yet after the raid on the Sheik Theater. He was at once elated because they needed the transportation themselves but worried because Rosie Shepherd was woefully behind schedule.

The Chevy slowed as Steel shot a glance over his

shoulder and said, "This mean Rosie's got trouble? Or what?"

"I hope not, Luther. Go slowly," Holden advised, but Luther Steel was already doing that.

David Holden looked back. None of the other vehicles in the convoy was that close to them that he could see it.

Holden could hear Luther Steel unlimbering his SIG from the DeSantis slant-shoulder rig. Holden put away the Beretta magazine and drew the Desert Eagle, clutching the .44 Magnum in his right fist as he leaned forward, ready to push Holly, the marine corps captain, down below the level of the dashboard for whatever safety that might provide.

They were eighteen-wheelers, three of them, as innocuous-looking as over-the-road transfer trucks could be, parked in the lot outside the abandoned printing plant. Mitch Diamond had provided them, complete with dummy loads that would mask the presence of people inside, weight-compensated and with proper legal manifests for the inevitable roadblocks.

Once everyone was boarded, until the PSF occupied the city at least, there was an excellent chance of getting out of Metro unmolested.

At least David Holden told himself that.

Luther Steel said, "I'm making the signal with the headlights."

"If they don't signal back, reverse out of here fast," Holden responded.

Steel only nodded.

Holden heard LeFleur drawing his SIG from its holster, a DeSantis rig like Steel wore.

David Holden's palms were sweating. The marine captain moaned softly in her pain. "Rest easy, Holly," Holden told her, putting a hand on her shoulder.

Lights blinked back from the nearest of the three semis.

David Holden stepped out of the car, the pad still Velcroed over the Chevy's dome light.

As loudly as he could, Holden whistled the recognition signal from the old television Western drama.

He waited.

The door of the semi that had blinked back opened, no dome light either.

"It's somethin' about Saturday nights and some other old TV show, David?"

It was Tommy Kellogg, a good man, a loyal Patriot but possessed of a memory that was indescribably poor.

"Yeah," Holden called back across the parking lot. "Something like that," David Holden, holstering the Desert Eagle but keeping his hand on it, limped across the lot toward Tommy Kellogg as Kellogg dropped down from the truck cab. When Holden was close enough that he wouldn't have to shout, he asked, "Where's Rosie?"

Kellogg spat some tobacco juice and answered, "They ran into some PSF and killed 'em all—I mean, Rosie's people killed all the PSF, you know? Anyways, threw 'em off their schedule. Two of Rosie's people—Fred and Harlan—bought it. She sent two more back with the bodies and the guns and shit they liberated from the dead PSF guys and went ahead."

"Only twelve people, then," Holden grunted. "Damn."

If he tried to put together a backup unit and charged into the tunnels, all sorts of bad possibilities loomed—from alerting the PSF to bumping into Rosie's people on the way out of the tunnels in near pitch-blackness. Radio was useless in the tunnels and might also alert the PSF, not to mention any FLNA that might still be around down there. "I shouldn't have—" Holden started to say, "let her go," but didn't. She was as good at this sort of thing as he was. Sometimes he thought she was better at it, although she'd never admit that.

There was nothing he could do but wait, and time left to get out of Metro was running out.

Holden looked at his watch. He'd give her one hour. Then he'd get the wounded military officers into one of the trucks and go into the tunnel system with Steel and the two people Rosie'd detailed to body recovery and carting out the captured weapons.

Holden closed his eyes, tried to control his pulse beat.

Chapter Thirty-Seven

*T*hey were halfway up the stairs leading from the subway station. Rose Shepherd gave the order to Randy Blumenthal as she pulled the muffs into place protecting her ears. "Fire!"

Blumenthal stepped farther out into the stairwell, the Hawk MM-1 grenade launcher at his hip. He fired the first round up the stairwell, then a second and third and fourth, and Rose Shepherd lost count as, squinting despite the protective goggles, she charged up the stairs, Bill Runningdeer on the right-hand side of the stairwell, leading his people up too.

Their only hope from the outset of the operation had been surprise, and as she reached the head of the stairs she realized they had achieved that. Two guards, one on his knees, the other on his back, eyes shut, hands over their ears. She could tell that they were screaming only by the way their mouths moved.

Rose Shepherd shot one of the men in the head with the M-16, Bill Runningdeer killing the other. Blumenthal was at the head of the stairs now, reloading the grenade launcher, this time, she knew, with gas.

Rose Shepherd tore off her goggles, pulled the gas mask from its pouch over her left breast, and pulled it on, her ears ringing as the whistling of the sound-and-light grenades still lingered.

She reached to her web gear, the M-16 shifted into her left hand, pulled one of the hand-thrown smoke grenades from her gear, lobbed it down the short hall-way stretching before her, shouted to Blumenthal, "Hit 'em, Randy!" Bill Runningdeer tossed a smoke grenade down the hallway immediately after hers as Blumenthal dropped to one knee and braced the grenade launcher.

Randy Blumenthal fired the Hawk straight down the center of the hallway, his first gas-grenade detonation in the next instant after the smoke grenades.

Rose Shepherd took the left side of the hall, Bill Runningdeer the right, Blumenthal firing another three gas grenades, then falling in behind Rose's team as they advanced.

At the end of the hall, it was almost impossible to see anything, but she had a plan of the Sheik Theater committed to memory, including its alterations for use by the PSF, one of the men rescued from the fair-grounds internment camp a veteran of "questioning" in the basement torture chamber.

Rose shouted to Runningdeer, "Stickin' to plan. Let's go!"

Behind her and along the file of Runningdeer's team, her orders were echoed and reechoed, one man from her team plus two men from Runningdeer's team falling back to hold the hall and the stairwell while Runningdeer and three of his men joined Rose and three of her men, running off toward the left of the hall through which they'd entered the Sheik's subbasement, toward the stairwell leading up to the actual basement.

At the base of the stairs—there was a heavy door at the top—they paused, one of the men from Runningdeer's team reaching into the American Indian ex-FBI man's backpack, pulling out the charge there as one of Rose's men took the charge from her backpack.

Blumenthal shouted, "Ready."

Rose ordered, "Go for it!" The two Patriots with the explosive charges ran up the stairwell, Blumenthal covering them with the Hawk MM-1, the first two rounds up, according to plan, high explosive.

Rose had the M-16 cheeked to her gas-masked face, waiting.

One charge was set on the doorframe, the second on the door, plastique—some of the precious little the Patriots had been able to steal from the FLNA—with timer detonators.

"Set!" one of the Patriots who'd planted the charges called out, along with the other man, running down the stairwell.

Blumenthal fell back, Rose and Runningdeer and the rest of the two teams doing the same.

". . . seven . . . six . . . five . . ." Rose Shepherd held her breath as the man beside her now continued the count. ". . . two . . . one!"

The floor and the walls—polished stone—seemed to vibrate around them, dust falling in clouds over them, chunks of the door and the doorframe rocketing past them out of the stairwell.

"Randy!" Rose screamed.

Blumenthal dropped to one knee and aimed the Hawk around the corner of the wall behind which they'd taken cover.

He fired the first high-explosive round, then the second, drawing back as the first detonation came, a cloud of dust and smoke belching down the stairwell. Rose Shepherd grabbed for one of the gas grenades on her gear, Runningdeer from the opposite side of the stairwell doing the same. "Now!" Rose shouted, Rose and Bill Runningdeer tossing the grenades up the stairwell in almost perfect synchronization.

Blumenthal stepped into the center of the stairwell base, crouched, fired the Hawk MM-1, gas grenades this time, the remainder of the twelve-round cylinder filled with them, emptying it as Rose Shepherd and the three men in her team started up the left side of the stairwell at a run, Bill Runningdeer and his three men doing the same.

The doorway was almost blocked with debris as she reached it, flipped a smoke grenade through, then sprayed a burst from her M-16 over the pile and started over, Runningdeer beside her.

As they dropped down, Runningdeer shouted, "On the right!"

Rose sidestepped left to be clear of Runningdeer, swinging the second M-16 forward as she did, firing the first one toward a knot of PSF personnel clustered around three overturned desks, Runningdeer's Uzi firing out, Rose Shepherd bringing up the second M-16, firing three-and four-round bursts as she and Runningdeer edged away from the entryway.

More of the Patriots spilled over the pile of debris, one of the men—she couldn't tell identities that clearly with the clouds of smoke and gas and everyone wearing a gas mask—taking a hit to the leg, stumbling, still firing.

She heard Blumenthal shout, "Outta my way!"

As she dove to cover behind a partially demolished partition wall—it might have been the wall for the men's lounge—Blumenthal fired the grenade launcher.

The explosion came, chunks of debris collapsing from the ceiling above them and the walls around them, the dust thick enough to cover their clothes and masks in a thin coating of gray.

There was no more resistance, for the moment.

"Bill! Hit those holding cells!"

"Gotchya!"

Runningdeer and his three men started out across the basement.

Rose Shepherd looked at Blumenthal. "Randy. We're on!"

He was already reloading.

Sirens were blaring in the night.

Overhead, David Holden thought he heard the sounds of helicopter gunships. He imagined them all converging on the Sheik Theater.

Something had to have gone wrong.

He looked at his watch. Forty minutes remained of the hour he had allotted.

"Anythin' wrong?" Kellogg asked.

"No." David Holden started back to one of the station wagons to help move another of the wounded into the semi Kellogg would drive. "Rosie can handle things perfectly well," Holden added, hoped.

Through the open first-floor doorway Rose Shepherd threw every grenade on her gear—gas, fragmentation, and smoke. Blumenthal fired the MM-1 as fast as he could trigger a round, the three other men spraying their M-16s through the doorway into what had once been the main floor of the theater, PSF personnel there hiding behind desks, trying to flee through the exit doors, going down in the storm of death.

Rose Shepherd swung an M-16 forward from her side and sprayed out the magazine, changing sticks, firing out the assault rifle again.

Twenty-nine minutes remained. The injured officers were loaded as were the weapons Rosie's unit had taken in the battle there in the tunnels with the PSF.

David Holden looked away from his watch.

It would take approximately twelve minutes to exit the Sheik Theater and reach the egress point from the tunnels near the parking lot where Holden waited.

It would take just that long for him to take a small group—

"What's on your mind?"

David Holden turned and looked at Luther Steel. "Rosie."

"You're thinking about going after her, right?"

"It crossed my mind." Holden nodded, lighting a cigarette. Sirens were still loud on the night air.

"So?"

"So?"

"Why haven't you done it already?"

"I've got faith in her. I mean, she's a woman, I'm a guy. I'm supposed to do all the rough-and-tough stuff and take care of her, but she's just as much the leader of the Metro Patriot cell as I am, maybe more so, although she'd never say that."

"No. You're the leader, David," Steel said slowly. "And she knows that. And if she's in trouble or even if she's not, she's banking on you doing the right thing, regardless of the fact that you love her. So what's the right thing?"

Holden looked at the Rolex on his left wrist again.

He inhaled on the cigarette.

He didn't answer Luther Steel, but he knew they both knew the answer—wait.

Chapter Thirty-Eight

*T*here probably were some PSF personnel still alive inside the Sheik Theater, but hunting them down and killing them wasn't worth the bother right now, nor were the confiscated civilian weapons stored in the balconies above—too much volume for too little utility.

Three M-16s taken from dead PSF personnel cradled in each arm and two more, besides her own, slung to her back, Rose Shepherd trudged down the stairwell toward the subbasement.

Bill Runningdeer met her at the base of the stairs. "We got—here, let me take some of those." He took three of the rifles from her, leaned them against the wall as she unburdened herself of the other three from her right arm. "We freed fifteen prisoners. Nine of them are healthy enough to walk on their own. One of them has to be carried—electric shock and beatings. That means we've got three extra people to carry out weapons with the two we'll need to carry that one injured man."

"Give each of those nine who can walk two rifles and two pistols apiece."

Runningdeer looked doubtful.

"There's no choice," Rose told him. "Send them out into the tunnels with three of our people loaded down with all they can carry. Get those five guys going on carrying weapons. Hurry."

She started back up the stairs in a dead run.

Fifteen minutes.

"Am I cutting it too close?" David Holden addressed the remark to the night or to the sky or, maybe, to God. He stood near the tunnel egress point, alone, the trucks a good hundred yards from him and no one else in hearing distance.

He understood, maybe just a little, how Rosie had felt when the FLNA had grabbed him and kidnapped him to Latin America, how she'd felt not knowing for a time if he was alive or dead.

Fourteen minutes.

He was running out of cigarettes. "Rosie. Come on, damn it!"

Holden stared into the abandoned storefront beneath which lay the tunnel egress. He waited.

Her arms loaded with captured weapons, Rose Shepherd was starting for the stairwell leading from the lobby level, the smell of tear gas still foul on the air, the dust stronger. For the last three minutes, men and equipment—Metro police and PSF—had been surrounding the theater.

Randy Blumenthal and Bill Runningdeer ran from the observation post she'd had them establish by the interior lobby doors.

"They're getting ready to rush us," Runningdeer called out as he ran.

Rose Shepherd nodded, raised her voice to the men going down the stairwell and to the men coming up. "We've gotten all we can. Down the stairs and out. We blow the subway station in sixty seconds!"

Rose Shepherd handed off half the load of M-16s

carried cradled in her arms to one of the freed political prisoners who had been coming back up the stairs for a fresh load.

"Let's boogie," she advised, taking the stairs down in a run.

At the base of the stairs two more men—Patriots—were coming back for more weapons. "We're evacuating," she told them. "Get everybody out past the subway station and started back along the tunnels. Now."

One of the men nodded, taking some of the M-16s from her arms.

David Holden and Luther Steel crouched in the darkness inside the stairwell leading to the basement of the abandoned clothing store.

Holden heard movement below.

The wall of the clothing store ran for some thirty to thirty-five feet in either direction from a storeroom doorway, beyond that doorway a large storage area about half the size of the display floor. There was a manhole cover leading into electrical and plumbing access for the store. Through that access chamber the tunnels were reached.

Holden looked at Steel, then started down the stairs, running toward the storeroom doorway.

Steel took the other side.

Holden heard voices, movement.

David Holden kicked open the doorway and crossed left to right, Steel crossing behind him right to left.

Across the sights of the Desert Eagle in the beam of the full-sized Maglite, Holden recognized faces, Patriots' faces, the faces of known political prisoners. One of these might even be the man who had witnessed what had happened to the rest of the officers on the train from which Lieutenant Barnabas Wood had escaped.

But Rosie wasn't among them.

* * *

Rose Shepherd gave the order. "Detonate!"

Bill Runningdeer touched the electrical leads together from the alligator-clipped battery and ran, Rose Shepherd beside him, Randy Blumenthal standing at the end of the station floor where the subway station dissolved into tunnel.

As they cleared in a dead run Blumenthal fired the Hawk MM-1, but already the crackle of explosions from the improvised demolition rig was starting its work.

Blumenthal was still firing the Hawk, high-explosive rounds, when Rose Shepherd screamed at him, "Randy! Run for it!"

Chunks of that beautiful ceiling that would be lost forever were crashing down around her as she ran, jumping from the end of the floor into the tunnel just below, Runningdeer right behind her.

Blumenthal. She looked back, saw him running. A chunk of the ceiling struck him, he stumbled, he lurched on toward the end of the floor, half falling, Runningdeer catching him, Rose catching the MM-1.

She turned it toward the station, firing once more.

The only subway station beneath Metro and, with it, access from the Sheik into the tunnel system would be sealed forever.

Holding the Hawk, three M-16s, plus her own two slung to her body, she ran as fast as she could pick up her feet, Runningdeer, with Blumenthal clinging to him, just ahead of her.

David Holden heard the explosions, one right after the other, like a string of immensely powerful firecrackers popping in series.

"Stay here!" David Holden shouted to Luther Steel. "And get everybody aboard the trucks! And the guns too!" Holden vaulted to the ladder within the manhole shaft, the Desert Eagle holstered, the flashlight—the beam zigzagged crazily as he climbed downward—stuffed into his belt.

When he hit the base of the shaft, he grabbed for the light.

Old bricks were scattered about on the floor. A rat scurried past his combat-booted feet.

Holden ducked through the opening in the brick wall and ran, shifting the flashlight to his left hand, the Desert Eagle in his right.

The tunnel was crashing down behind them, but the effect slowing.

She kept running, catching up with Runningdeer, grabbing Randy Blumenthal's right arm and pulling it over her shoulder, Blumenthal between Runningdeer and herself now.

"Come on!"

She kept running.

David Holden reached a bend in the tunnel. The sounds of the explosions were dying but still loud enough that he could tell which of the two shafts—the right or the left—to take.

He took the right shaft, running.

The trucks should have gone by now, she told herself, should have followed her orders and waited until the bulk of the men were out with the bulk of the weapons, waited a little longer and when no one else appeared, driven like hell.

But once they were free of the tunnels, Rose Shepherd told herself, she and Runningdeer and Blumenthal would have a chance.

"Come on!" Maybe they'd disobeyed orders, the

truck drivers, like Tommy Kellogg. Maybe they were waiting.

Blumenthal was moving under his own power now.

Each of them held a flashlight, the beams from the lights dancing wildly over the tunnel floor.

David Holden tripped, caught himself, ran.

He saw light.

"Rosie!" It was crazy to yell in the tunnels. What if it was the PSF? "Rosie!"

"David!" It wasn't Rosie.

"Danny?" Danny Klein was one of the Patriots from Rosie's group. Holden kept running, almost blinded by the half-dozen flashlights beaming toward him. "Turn 'em away, huh! Where's Rosie?"

"She should be right behind us. They were blowin' the—"

"Never mind," Holden ordered. "Get the hell outta here. Now!"

David Holden slipped past them in the tunnel, more faces he recognized, more faces of freed political prisoners.

He was tempted to run back and borrow an M-16, for his had been destroyed earlier when the receiver took a bullet. There wasn't time. He kept running, aware of the pain in his left thigh only remotely, as if the leg weren't really attached to him.

His hand sweated on the Desert Eagle's pebble-textured grip.

His gloves were in his BDUs.

"Rosie!"

No answer. He was out of the sewer-tunnel access and into the abandoned subway tunnels now, the debris the only noticeable difference. In the darkness beyond the beam of his flashlight, red pinpoints that were rats' eyes stared at him.

He kept running, tripping again, catching himself. "Rosie!"

Holden stopped dead, thinking he heard a voice. "Rosie!"

He listened, holding his breath, suddenly storming with rage within him against the drip-dropping of water, the scurrying feet of rats. "Rosie!"

"David!"

David Holden started running again, toward the sound of her voice.

The air within the cocoon of boxes inside the trailer of the eighteen-wheeler was warm and stale and smelled of body odor and drying sweat.

Twice as many people as the hiding place was designed for were secreted within it. But David Holden was happy for the opportunity to sit so close to Rosie, his arms around her shoulders.

Around them squatted many of the men freed from the Sheik Theater, those who were at least capable of sitting. Others lay sprawled in exhaustion or pain or both. One of these latter was Elmer Fulton. He was the man Julie had spoken of, the man who would have been on observation duty at the train yard when Lieutenant Barnabas Wood and the female air force officer had made their escape.

But Elmer Fulton was unconscious now.

The fate of the men from that train, if Elmer Fulton knew it, was still a mystery.

Holden glanced at his watch. They had passed the last checkpoint five minutes ago, were on their way out of Metro. In another few minutes he could actually consider them safe, at least for the moment.

Holden held Rosie a little more tightly, whispering to her, "I love you."

She leaned her head against his chest.

www.ingramcontent.com/pod-product-compliance
Lightning Source LLC
Chambersburg PA
CBHW021458250626
47154CB00004BA/1430